WAPITI WIDOW

ROCKY MOUNTAIN SAINT BOOK 7

B.N. RUNDELL

WOLFPACK
PUBLISHING
— EST 2013 —

Wapiti Widow
(Rocky Mountain Saint Book 7**)**
B.N. Rundell

Paperback Edition
© Copyright 2018 B.N. Rundell

Wolfpack Publishing
6032 Wheat Penny Avenue
Las Vegas, NV 89122

Paperback ISBN: 978-1-64119-439-6
eBook ISBN: 978-1-64119-438-9

Library of Congress Control Number: 2018961454

WAPITI WIDOW

CHAPTER ONE
FAMILY

TATE STARED AT THE SLOW RISING FULL MOON THAT DANCED its way between the few wispy clouds that hung in the eastern sky. High above glimmered one lonely star, it's lantern well-lit in the dusky sky as if it was paving the way for his companions. This was one of Tate's favorite times. Sitting on the porch, enjoying the coming darkness and listening to the sounds of the night. The cicadas were tuning up their ratcheting instruments, and a single nighthawk was sounding its warning to some predator that threatened its nest. A solitary coyote, not too far away, began his mating yipping in hopes of a romantic night. Tate's favorite sound of the mountains wouldn't be heard this night as it was too early in the season for the bull elk to bugle their challenges. But another sound came and made him smile, it was the voices of his two children telling their mother good night and sleep tight. The door pushed open, the light steps of his redhead came to his side and a soft touch to his shoulder spoke more than words could say.

Tate Saint lifted his hand to take her fingers as she pirou-etted around in front of his chair to take her place in the rocker beside him. Maggie, the strong-willed Irish lass that had become his wife just a little over ten years past and blessed this family with two fine children. Sean Michael was going on ten and his wee sister was trying to force her way to six. Sean was looking like his Pa, dark wavy hair, and a frame that showed promise of wide shoulders, narrow hips and eyes that glinted with strong character. And the girl, Sadie, was a spitting image of her mother, long red hair that seemed to shine golden in the sunlight, fair complexion with a herd of freckles that chased one another across her nose. Her eyes sparkled with mischief and her mind was quicker than a scared rabbit and it was all her parents could do to stay ahead of her.

As Maggie leaned back in her rocker, she looked at her husband's face with the moonlight showing the beginnings of wrinkles and she grinned. But when Tate leaned his head back and looked at her, she had to ask, "And what are you smiling about, Mr. Saint?"

His chest bounced as he chuckled, "Oh, just rememberin' the first time I saw you and you started flirtin' with me."

"Flirting with you? I did no such thing! The way I remember it I couldn't get a moment to myself an' I did'na have an inkling of what you were up to, followin' me around like ye were. And you kept talkin' all the while, you did."

"Talkin'? Me? I couldn't get a word in edgewise, and when I did it was just to say 'shush' cuz you was makin' such a racket I thought you were gonna get ever' Injun in the country down on us an' wantin' to take that red hair for their scalp lance."

Maggie playfully slapped at Tate's arm and giggled at his remarks. "An' it's been 'most of eleven years since we started lookin' for me father."

Tate smiled and said, "Did I ever thank him for gettin' lost so you'd come lookin' for him?"

Maggie giggled at the thought, remembering the first time they met at Bent's Fort and Tate agreed to take her to search for her father, a man that left his family to search for gold in the Rockies and hadn't been heard from in years. They found him in the Bayou Salado, and more than that, they found each other and made life-long friends among the Ute people in the process. Her father, Michael Patrick O'Shaunessy, also found love and married Little Otter of the Yamparika Ute.

Tate looked at the big moon and remembered, "Eleven years, hard to believe, it seems like yesterday. When my Pa died and I came to the mountains, I was a still-wet-behind-the-ears pup, and if it hadn't been for Kit Carson, I don't think I'da survived even one winter. And as I remember, it was Kit that insisted I take you to find your father." He let a smile crease his face and added, "Guess I need ta thank him too, ya reckon?"

"The way I remember it, you thanked both my Pa and Kit more than once," answered Maggie, using her toe to set the rocker moving. She reached her hand across to take Tate's and the two enjoyed the moment in the moonlight.

A big owl asked his question of the night and Tate said, "Maggie, that's who!"

The redhead smiled at him and said, "And what was the question?"

"Didn't you hear? He said, 'Who, who, who's for you? And I tol' him."

Maggie smiled and said, "You know, if somebody would have told me all those years ago, that I would find my love in the mountains of the Rockies and that I would raise a family in the wilderness and be happier than I ever thought possible, I would'na believed a word of it."

"Nor I. When I left Missouri and headed to the far blue mountains, my only thought was to get to the mountains, build a cabin and live in the wild. I just hadn't thought past that, and yet, there has been so much." He shook his head as he remembered, "I never imagined becoming friends with so many of the Native people, the Kiowa, Comanche, the Caputa and Yamparika Ute, not to mention the many mountain men and others. If I tried to write it down, it'd probably never be believed."

Maggie smiled at the memories, stood and walked to the porch rail, leaned out to look at the golden orb and turned back to look at her man. His smooth-shaven face was marked by his dark eyes that always held a mystery, a dimple on his right cheek accented the smile lines from his ever present and pleasant expression. His broad shoulders were wider than the chair back, yet his slim hips fit the seat with room to spare. Although his appearance was one of leanness, his strength always surprised her for she had seen him single-handedly lift the box of a loaded wagon to allow a wheel to be replaced. His wavy dark hair hung to the collar of his buckskin shirt, pushed back on the sides behind his ears and his broad forehead showed strength and even wisdom. She was proud of her man and every time she looked at him, her heart fluttered at the thought that she was the only woman that ever knew or would know the pleasure of being held in those strong arms.

Tate dropped his hand to the side of the chair and he absent-mindedly stroked the fur at the neck of his long-time companion, Lobo. The big wolf had become his friend even before he knew Maggie and had saved his bacon on more than one occasion. "And if somebody told me that I would be so blessed as to have a spit-fire redhead that was beautiful to boot as my wife and the mother of my children, well, I wouldn't have believed it. Or if they said I'd have a wolf for a pet, a bear for a friend, and a wonderful life with an amazing family, it just wouldn't have seemed possible."

He stood and walked to his bride and with hands at her waist, he pulled her to him and took advantage of the moonlight as he kissed her passionately. When they leaned back to look at one another and take a much-needed breath, Maggie's smile lit up the night when he saw the sparkle of starlight reflected in the green Irish eyes and he kissed her again. The cicadas started their chorus and the big old owl asked his question once again to be answered by Maggie, "You, that's who!" as she pointed her finger and poked Tate's chest, smiling. "And we better turn in, because you promised to fix my garden spot in the morning. I want to get the seeds planted and have a good harvest this year, and I can't do that if we spend all our time 'moonin' on the porch!"

"Oh, alright, if you're gonna be like that. I guess we better go to bed," he answered, shoulders dropping as if he was dejected beyond description. But he turned back to smile at his redhead with a slightly mischievous glint in his eye as he nodded for her to join him. He held the door open for her and swatted her on the rear as she walked past. She feigned shock, but her smile said otherwise.

CHAPTER TWO
HOME

"Oh, Pa, it's beautiful! I didn't know you were makin' one for me!" The boy beamed with delight as he fingered the finely crafted bow. "It's just like yours, ain't it?"

Tate smiled as he nodded and then corrected his son, "You better not let your Ma hear you talk like that, she'd blister us both!"

Sean knew immediately how he erred and corrected himself, "*Isn't* it! It's just like yours, *isn't* it?" He had yet to take his eyes from the smooth wood, rawhide wrapped grip, and carved nocks of the youth sized longbow. The boy had often admired the longbow that his father used and that earned him the Indian name of Longbow. His father had often told him, after considerable urging by the boy, about the history of the longbow and how it was used by the warriors of England and Wales for hundreds of years in their battles with would be conquerors. "It has greater strength or power and in the hands of a skilled archer, the arrow has been known to pierce their enemies' mail, or woven steel armor. A longbow has greater draw weight than a traditional Indian bow and can send an arrow farther and with greater accuracy," were the words remembered by Sean as he looked to his Pa and asked, "Is this more powerful than an Indian bow?"

Tate smiled at the enthusiasm of his son, "It is more powerful than the usual bow that young men use, but the bow of an adult would probably be just as powerful as that one. But, it's gonna take you a while to master it. It's not like your mother's that you've used before, so let's start learning, shall we?"

"Sure Pa, I wanna learn!" He lifted the bow with the left hand on the grip and the right on the string, looked to his father for an arrow, hoping to start shooting right away.

"Well, first, you need to learn about stringing and unstringing your bow. Whenever it's not in use, you must unstring it so the wood won't lose it strength. Now . . ." and he set about demonstrating how to manipulate the string by using his own bow and waiting for the boy to follow his instructions.

"That's right, step through the bow and with your right foot to hold the nock, use the other leg and your hand to pull the upper limb or stave down to loosen the string," he demonstrated on his own, and watched as Sean mimicked his movements, struggling a mite, but finally able to remove the string from the nock. When he succeeded, Tate said, "Good, now do the same thing to string it."

After several times of the boy nocking, and unstringing the bow, Tate said, "Alright, now, you've seen me use my bow, and you've seen your mother use hers and some of our friends use theirs, do you know what the difference is?"

"Uh, yeah, they hold this arm straight," and he extended his left arm with the bow until it was straight, "and they pull back on the string and arrow," and he started to pull on the string of his bow but was surprised at how difficult it was and looked at his father for an explanation.

Tate chuckled at the exasperation of his son, knowing the

boy expected to immediately master the weapon and go hunting. They left the house early and were now down in the flats between the creek and the tree line and the boy thought they were going hunting for some fresh meat. Tate's purpose for bringing the bows away from the clearing before the house was to demonstrate to his son just how far a longbow could be effectively used. "Now, watch what I do, and see if you can tell the difference." The man held the bowstring by his cheekbone, then stepped forward extending his left arm, but using the strength of his entire body to bring the bow to a full draw. He held it for a moment, and spoke to the boy, "This is what they call 'bending the bow'." He went on to explain, "You see, Sean, a longbow has a draw weight of well over a hundred pounds, while a traditional bow will usually only be about fifty to sixty pounds."

"What does mine have?" asked the boy, looking at his new weapon.

"Well, best I can tell, yours has about the same as a traditional bow. But the usual youth bow would only be about thirty to thirty-five pounds of draw weight. What that means is it would take that much weight to pull the string down if the bow were suspended between two points and the weight applied to the string. That's a good way to determine the strength of the bow and what it can do with an arrow. Now, you try it."

Tate helped the boy practice 'bending the bow' by using his weight and strength as he stepped into the bow. After several tries, Sean was certain he was ready, and his father relented. His first attempt with an arrow sent the shaft wobbling away and landing in the grass about thirty yards away. He looked to his Pa for approval, and Tate grinned, "That was pretty good for your first try. Now, here's three more arrows, see what you can do."

"What do I shoot at, Pa?" he asked as he nocked an arrow and looked to his teacher.

"That clump of sage, just beyond where your arrow went, try to put them into that clump."

Each arrow went just a little further than the previous one and the last barely cleared the top of the clump and stuck in the grass just beyond. Sean looked back at his Pa and said, "I did it!" He grinned as his father nodded his head, smiling.

"Now, you need to fetch those arrows."

Sean nodded and started to step out but paused, "Pa, how far will your bow shoot?"

"Uh, quite a bit further than that, that's only 'bout thirty, thirty-five yards."

"Could you show me? Huh?"

Tate looked at the expectant expression on the boy's face and nodded as he pulled an arrow from the quiver at his belt. He looked in the direction of the sage and told the boy, "See that sage you were shooting at?" The boy nodded and looked back at his Pa. "I'm going to shoot over that and beyond. See where those willows are at the bend of the creek, yonder?"

"Yeah, but Pa, that's a long ways!" declared the youngster.

"Yup, that bend in the creek is about a hundred and fifty yards. Now, you'll have to watch close, cuz when an arrow goes that far, it's hard to see." He nocked an arrow, lifted the bow, and in one easy motion, stepped into the bow and when at full draw, he loosed the shaft that whispered away. If it weren't for the feathered fletching, the arrow would not be seen, but it went well beyond the bend and easily cleared the willows to land out of sight.

Sean stood mesmerized as he let out his breath with a whispered, "Wow!"

Tate had watched the flight of the shaft and looked down at the boy and back to the creek, "Wow, is right. Get down, boy!" he demanded as he put his hand on Sean's shoulder. They both dropped to their knees and Sean looked to his Pa to see where he was looking. In the distance, standing erect beside the willows, was a massive grizzly. He cocked his head and let out an angry roar that challenged anything in his domain and reverberated from the hillside, bouncing as a muffled echo into the range beyond and seeming to pierce the very bones of the boy and his Pa. Sean looked at his Pa, who had already nocked another arrow, but stayed on his one knee, waiting. With his free hand, he held a finger to his lips to quiet the boy, and then looked to the edge of the trees where their horses were tethered. As always, it was with a loop that would keep them but allow them to pull free if necessary. And pull free they did, and fled through the trees, headed home to safety and as far away from the bear as possible.

Tate chuckled and shook his head, bringing his eyes back to the protesting beast. The bear let loose another complaint, dropped to all fours swinging his head side to side and growling his protests. Satisfied nothing was going to accept the challenge, the big boar turned away and moseyed into the trees. Tate waited a few moments, making sure the bear wasn't changing his mind, and when satisfied, he stood and gave a hand to his boy.

"Wow, Pa, that bear was big!" declared the excited boy. "I saw you nock an arrow, would your bow have been enough to kill it?"

"Well, since it was the only weapon we had available, I had to be ready in case he charged, but a well-placed arrow would at least make him think charging wasn't a good idea. But, it would probably take more'n one to stop him. Once a bear starts his charge, especially one that big, it takes a lot to stop 'em. And when they're down on all fours and charging, it's hard to hit a kill spot. But right now, we need to start walkin' since the horses already went home on their own."

Sean's shoulders dropped as he looked to the spot where the horses had been tethered and back to his Pa, shook his head and started off. It was an easy walk, less than two miles to take them back to the cabin and once in the clearing, Sean started running, anxious to show his Ma the new bow. "Look Ma! Look what Pa made for me!" he declared, taking the porch steps two at a time.

Maggie examined the bow, feigned surprise, and looked at her happy son as he beamed with pride. "It's a fine bow. But can you shoot it?"

"Sure Ma, I can shoot it. And I did too, but you shoulda seen Pa. He shot so far, I couldn't even see where the arrow went, but I sure saw that grizzly though!"

"Grizzly?! You saw a grizzly?" she looked from Sean to Tate, now climbing the steps with a mischievous grin. "When the horses came home, I looked them over for blood and when I found none, I thought they just got loose, but a grizzly?"

"Yup, a big 'un, too. He stood, oh, maybe nine feet tall. I'm surprised you didn't hear him roar all the way up here," he stated matter-of-factly as he plopped into his chair. Maggie had already unsaddled and corralled the horses and he was glad he could just sit and rest for a moment.

"Where were you and how close to the house is this bear?" she asked, grilling the pair for details.

"Ah, we were clear down in the flats, outta the timber, an' when he took off, he was headed to the tall timber, thataway," he answered as he waved his hand over his right shoulder.

Maggie leaned forward and stood from her rocker, surprising Lobo in the process who lifted his head to see what was happening. She went into the cabin without a word and came right back with a Hawken in her hands, stood it beside the door and sat back down.

Tate looked at his woman, at the rifle and back at Maggie as he asked, "Is that for the grizzly or me?"

Maggie crossed her arms and shrugged her shoulders as she answered, "For whichever one needs it first!"

CHAPTER THREE
VISITOR

THE CLATTER OF HOOVES FROM DOWN IN THE TREES BROUGHT Tate to his feet and reaching for the Hawken. His possibles bag and powder horn hung from the peg beside the rifle and he draped those around his neck and shoulder, motioning for Maggie and Sean to go into the house. With a hand signal, he brought Lobo to his side and the two silently moved from the porch and into the timber to take his vigil from an oft-used position behind some downed timber near a towering ponderosa. He knew the sounds came from the Sand Creek trail below and south of the cabin, but what he didn't know was if they were friends or enemies. He dropped to one knee, bringing the muzzle of the rifle to rest on the log before him while Lobo stood with head lowered, searching the trees. The wolf let a low rumbling growl tell Tate he had seen the intruders but was waiting for his pack leader to make his move. Tate eared back the hammer, visually checked the cap on the nipple, and lowered his cheek to the stock, waiting.

His first sight was of a mounted buckskin clad man, but there were several animals and he wanted to see who the others were. As the trail opened a mite to give a clear view, Tate recognized the grizzled old man from Hardscrabble. Alexander Barclay was a trader from the little settlement on the far side of the Wet Mountains and with Tate's help, had established a lucrative trade with the Caputa Ute in the foothills of the San Juan's. His trail always brought him over the Music Pass and near to Tate's cabin where he was always made welcome. Tate stood, "Hey old man! Whatchu doin' in my woods?"

"Wal, if it ain't the ol' Saint of the Rockies! I see you still got'chur hair!"

"Mine, an more besides! You sure do make a lotta racket when you go anywhere," responded Tate as he looked to the string of pack-mules that trailed behind his friend. "Whatchu doin'? Movin' yore whole tradin' post? I mean to say, with three loaded packmules, it looks like you're plannin' on tradin' them Ute outta everthin' they got!"

The man reined up beside Tate and after their greetings, gigged his mount forward as Tate walked alongside. "Wal, ain't all this fer them Utes, I figgered to unload some of it at yore place!"

"Now, what makes you think you got anything I want?"

He chuckled. "You just wait to see what I got. Yore woman got dinner ready yet?"

"That's the only reason you stop off here is to get a home-cooked meal."

"Hehehe, you got that right, sonny boy," cackled the old man. His buckskins were almost black with the wearing and the grease from his hands, knowing the grease from the fat drippings also helped the skins shed water. His fur hat was so old and worn, it was hard to tell what varmint sacrificed its pelt for the old man's topknot, and his whiskers gave evidence of liberal use of tobacco. But his eyes were lively and showed the mischief that made the man so likable. The trader's trips to the mountains had made it so the Saints made fewer trips to Bent's Fort for supplies, but he seldom had all they needed or wanted. Yet, his visits were always enjoyable, and the entire family had sort of adopted him as a favorite uncle.

When they came into the clearing before the house, Barclay spotted Maggie tending a pot at a fire away from the porch that sent a small spiral of smoke into the trees. She straightened up and waved as the trader and Tate started for the corrals to put up the animals for the night. "I see your woman prefers the outdoor fire at this time o' year."

"Yup, she likes to keep it cool in the house and when she's usin' a dutch oven, she says it's easier to tend to outside. That's why I made them benches yonder, to make it easy to sit a spell and enjoy the fire," explained Tate.

The men worked quickly to derig the animals and turn them into the corrals that now stood empty, save Tate's horse, Shady, and the boy's horse, Dusty. The other horses and mule had been turned out to pasture in the upper meadow and if needed, Tate would use Shady to bring them back down. When the mules were corralled, they rolled in the dirt and kicked up some dust, driving the men to the benches by the fire.

"Well, Mrs. Saint, I see you've been keepin' these rascals well fed!" declared Barclay as he seated himself on the log bench by the fire.

Maggie straightened up and with hands on hips she declared, "Somebody's got to look out for them. If they didn't have me tendin' and feedin' 'em, I do believe they'd starve themselves to death!" Her Irish brogue had been tainted by the many years in the wilderness and conversing with mountain men and Indians and she quite often lapsed into their vernacular. But if Sean or Sadie ever failed in their grammar she was quick to correct them. She noticed Sean staring at his mother and she added, "Sure'n me name is Maggie O'Shaunessy Saint, I be the glue what holds the lot o' these t'gether." She winked at Sean who leaned back beside his dad with a broad smile. "So, are ye just visitin' n' eatin' or did ye bring me some supplies like I asked ye to the last time ye came into these woods?"

"Wal, I got some mighty fine stuff for you all, but we'll wait till after the eatin' 'fore I break open them packs and dig it all out fer ya, an' I'm right shore you're gonna like whut I brung ya."

"As long as you brought my essentials, I'll be happy," answered Maggie as she turned back to the pot hanging over the fire. She used the lid lifter, stirred the fixin's and replaced the lid before stepping to the smaller dutch oven that held the cornbread. She lifted the lid, dropping the coals aside, and poked the cornbread to check its doneness, replaced the lid and scooped some hot coals atop the rimmed lid, before sitting on the bench with Tate.

Turning to Barclay, Tate asked, "So, who's the president now?"

"Who was it the last time ya knowed?" replied Barclay.

"Uh, some rascal named Fillmore, I think."

"Huh, nope, ain't him no more. It's a outlaw general name 'o Pierce, Franklin Pierce," spat Barclay.

"Well, from the way you're actin', you don't like him. What's the problem?"

"He's a northerner that's tryin' to tear up this country! Why, it used to be 'gainst the law fer slavery in these hyar territories, an' he went 'n pushed what they called the Kansas-Nebraska act and done away wit' th' Missouri compromise. Now, he done split the country west o' the mountains into Nebraska territory and Kansas territory an' the whole country's gettin' riled up 'bout slavery! I'm 'bout ready to pull up stakes an' head farther west ta' git away from them politicians!"

"Are you tellin' me these mountains behind us are the dividin' line for what'chur talkin' about?"

"Yup, they is that!"

Maggie had given the different pots of food another check, and interrupted the men with, "How 'bout you two hush with your politics and pick up a pot and let's go inside and eat?"

Both jumped to their feet and grabbed a pot, Sean picking the coolest one that had been set aside earlier, and all three carried the goodness into the house for their anticipated dinner. Once inside, they gathered around the table and at Tate's direction, they held hands as he prayed to give thanks to the Lord and to ask for His blessings.

As Maggie watched the men devour the smoked elk roast, potatoes, carrots, and onions with the side of beans and corn-bread, she smiled in satisfaction at their delight. She looked down at Sadie Marie and smiled as the girl did her best to keep up with her big brother. When all was done, Maggie brought out Tate's favorite Spider Cake, or peach cobbler, made in a cast iron skillet, and within moments the skillet was empty, and everyone sat back with contented smiles and full stomachs.

"Mrs. Saint, I must say, that is the finest meal I ever had, yes'm it shore is. And I thank you m'am from the bottom of my overstuffed belly!" declared Barclay, grinning through the thick beard. He stood and started outside and said, "It might be easier if'n y'all come on out with me cuz I ain't about to pack it in!"

Maggie started cleaning off the table and Tate stopped her with a motion for her to join them, and adding, "I'll help you with that later, let's see what he's got," and winked at her and stretched out his hand to take hers. They followed the trader and the two enthusiastic youngsters out the door and were soon beside the packs as Barclay started sorting through the loaded panniers and parfleches. He made it a point to shield his fumbling by having his back to the waiting family but soon turned around with a bundle for Maggie. He handed it to her and said, "For the lady o' the manor!" Maggie accepted the package and started undoing the twine tie. Her eyes lit up and she pulled out a corner of wool in the Irish Clover pattern of blue and green.

"Aye, 'n sure'n tis a beauty o' th' Irish Clover!" she declared as she fingered the wool.

Barclay smiled and turned back to the packs and set salt, sugar, a big bag of beans, four sticks of galena, three big tins of powder, a sizable bag of flour, and a pile of other necessities. He stood with hands on his hips and said, "So, did I bring what'cha needed?"

Maggie smiled and answered, "Aye, it looks like most ever'thing."

The trader slapped his forehead and turned back around, bent to another pannier and brought back a bag marked 'seeds'.

Maggie smiled even broader, "Now, you've made my day!"

Barclay smiled and turned back to the packs again and came up with a new rifle he held out to Tate. With wide eyes and his mouth open a tad, Tate accepted it with care, looking to fore and aft like a sailor setting out to sea. He lifted his eyes to Barclay, "A Sharps?" To which the trader nodded his head and watched the man take in every detail of the weapon. He dropped the lever to open the breech, pulled it shut and lifted the weapon to his shoulder to sight down the barrel. He looked to Barclay, "What caliber?"

"That there's a model 1853 in the .52 caliber. It'll shoot accurate out to, oh, 'bout a thousand yards!"

Tate looked at the man, surprised, and asked, "A thousand yards?"

"Yup, they're already callin' it the buffalo gun." He turned back to his pack and brought out a pistol and held it out to Tate. Tate leaned the rifle against the corral poles and accepted the pistol, to again marvel at the weapon before him. He lifted his face to the trader, showing raised eyebrows in a question.

Barclay smiled and said, "That's a Colt Dragoon in .41 caliber. An' I brung two extry cylinders fer it," and he lifted his other hand and said, "An' here's a littler one fer the Mrs." When Maggie stepped around her husband to see what was offered, she took hold of a pocket pistol, called a Baby Dragoon, and her marvel mirrored that of her husband's.

By the time the trading and bickering was all finished, Barclay had one empty pack-mule, the Saint family had a new arsenal and full cupboards, and Barclay had a heavier pouch at his belt. Everyone was happy when the trader loaded up the next day to start his journey to the Indian villages. "So, be sure to give Two Eagles and Red Bird our greetings and tell them to come see us, y'hear?"

"I'll shore do that, an' next time I come thru, mebbe you can get me set up wit' them Comanche to do a little tradin' down yonder way?"

"Be happy to, but they're not quite as friendly with outsiders as the Ute are, they've been burnt too many times, but they do go to Bent's on occasion, so they just might be willin' to trade with you. We'll see next time!" answered Tate as he stepped back beside Maggie to wave to the departing trader.

The old man, who was called old by just about everyone, was only about ten years Tate's senior, but the grey in his beard made him look a lot older, turned to wave to his friends and led his string of mules into the trees. This was a familiar route to him, since he opened trading with the Ute's several years back when Tate introduced him to Two Eagles, the leader of the Caputa Ute. Barclay would usually travel north along the tree line of the Sangre de Cristos until the valley narrowed, then he would cut across to the foothills of the San Juans. Like most mountain men, he didn't like traveling in the open country, and the San Luis Valley was wide open.

THE BOY WAS WALKING ON TIPTOES, ARMS FLAILING TO THE side as he fought to keep his balance, but it was pretty difficult to do, what with Sheriff Canterbury practically lifting him off the ground by one ear. "Ooowww, come on Sheriff, let me go! I didn't do nothin'!"

"You call that nothin'? You coulda got somebody killed when them mules stampeded with that wagon! All on accounta you shootin' off your homemade fireworks! I've had enuff o' your shenanigans, boy!" He was taking Reuben Ritter to his mother, Cora, who was the town's gunsmith and the owner of the only rooming house in the bustling town of St. Joseph, Missouri, the jumping off place for the many wagon trains heading west on the Oregon Trail.

The sheriff pushed open the door to see Cora Ritter busy at her workbench, her short grey hair going in every direction and doing little to hide her black piercing eyes that flared with anger when she saw her boy dancing at the end of the sheriff's pinching fingers. She ripped off the visor, the type usually seen on bookkeepers and bankers, and growled at the sheriff, "What's he done now?"

"He stampeded a team o' mules and the wagon they was pullin' and sent everybody on the street divin' behind water troughs, hitch rails, and anything else they could find. Now, the boy's mighty lucky there weren't nobody hurt an' no real damage done, 'cepin' fer the corner post on the balcony o'er the Blue Devil saloon and a couple o' Hazel's girls 'bout tumbled off. You know how they's allus advertisin' their wares up thar."

"It probly' done 'em good to get dunked in a water trough, them girls need a bath more often," answered the gravelly voice of Cora.

"Wal, that may be, but I've had 'bout 'nuff of this boy's monkeyshines. The next time, I'm gonna throw him in the hoosegow an' see if'n that'll teach that boy a lesson!" With that exclamation, the sheriff shoved Reuben towards his ma, releasing his grip on the boy's ear. Reuben stumbled, caught himself on the counter and turned with a snarl toward the sheriff, looking like a wildcat ready to pounce.

"BOY!" shouted his ma in the tone that all sons have heard from an angry mother. It stopped him in his tracks and made him straighten up to stare at his ma.

"But Ma!" started the boy but was stayed by her angry stare from beneath her furrowed brow. Her nostrils flared and her grip on the hammer tightened.

"I'll take care of it, Sheriff. You ain't gonna have no more trouble with him, that's for sure!" Her snarl made the sheriff back out of the shop without saying another word. When the door closed, she turned her attention to Reuben, "Looks like you dunnit this time, boy." She pointed her finger to the back door that led to the rooming house, "You go on back an' help your sister clean things up, an' don't you leave the house, understand?"

"Yeah Ma, I understand." His shoulders drooped as he marched to the door and into the rooming house. The building was one of the larger frame and brick structures in the town. It sat back from the river but afforded the guests with a view of all the activities of the ferry and the river from the back porch and balcony. Cora and her husband, Luther, had purchased the building and converted it to a combination shop and roomer with the money Cora inherited from her parents who died in the Cholera epidemic in St. Louis. But her husband had an incurable case of wanderlust and after just one year of trying to be a keeper of a rooming house and the husband of the only gunsmith in town, the news of the gold strike in California was all the motivation he needed to hightail it to the land of golden dreams.

He had only been gone a little over a year when she received a letter that told of the man's death in a saloon and the writer of the letter sent the $2.50 he had in his britches. It was all the man had after the undertaker took out his expenses. Cora had kept the news from her twins, Reuben and Rachel, using the possibility of their Pa's return as motivation for them to do as she instructed and help out around the business. But now she knew she was going to have to do more.

She hung the sign on the door that told of her return 'soon' and started down the street. She stepped into the bank and started to the railing the separated the desks from the teller cages. An uplifted hand by a young clerk stopped her with a curt, "May I help you, m'am?" as eyes looked her up and down with obvious disapproval.

Cora cocked her head to the side and looked at the young man and spoke slowly but condescendingly, "Look, you young whippersnapper, you'd have to be twice your age 'fore I'd even consider lettin' you hep me, but if you don't get back there an' tell ol' Boettcher that Cora's out here, I'll kick you so hard you won't be able to sit down fer a week. Now git!"

The young man, like so many other newcomers to St. Joe,

didn't know Cora and was astounded by her manner, and her temper scared him enough to make him slowly back away and answer, "Uh, yes m'am, right away, m'am."

When the tall but portly and dignified banker stepped from his office, holding his gold pocket watch that usually dangled on a chain that stretched across his ample belly, he looked to the grey-haired woman who stood wringing her gloves nervously. The banker forced a smile and announced, "Cora, to what do I owe the pleasure of your visit. Come, come, step into my office if you will." He held open the swinging gate that permitted entrance to the desk area and motioned to the open office door. "Go right in and have a seat."

He followed her in and she sat on the edge of the padded armchair and said, "J.W., you've been wantin' to get your hands on my place ever since you opened this here bank, right?"

"Well, yes, you do have a very desirable location and a good building, course it would require considerable repairs and investment and-"

"It don't require nothin'! Now, what's your best offer, an' make it a good 'un, cuz Hazel, o'er at the Blue Devil was wantin' it too!"

J.W. leaned forward to rest his arms on the desk and look more closely at Cora. "What has you so interested in selling? Is there something I should know?"

"Ain't none of yore business why, I'm just ready to light a shuck outta here. Now, what's yore offer?"

J.W. began scribbling on a piece of paper, writing numbers in columns, adding and scratching out, and then wrote down a number and turned the paper to Cora. She looked at it, turned to stare out the window for a moment, obviously calculating something in her mind, and turned back to the banker. She stood and stretched out her hand and said, "Done! I'm goin' down to the Livery to see Jake and get me a wagon. When I come back, you have the papers and money ready and we'll get this o'er with, deal?"

J.W. stood with a broad smile on his face and shook Cora's hand vigorously, "Absolutely, absolutely. I'll get the papers drawn up right away and all will be ready for you when you return."

Cora looked at him, half expecting him to express his thanks, but then reminded herself who she was talking to and dismissed the thought. J.W. followed her to the rail, opened the gate for her, and nodded with a smile as she passed him by to quickly make her exit. As she left the bank, she turned down the street and started to the Livery. Jake Thurgood had been a good friend and had come to St. Joe about the same time as Cora and her family. His livery business was booming with so many using St. Joe as a jumping off point for wagon trains to take to the Oregon Trail, and he was well supplied.

When Cora stepped through the big doors, she paused to let her eyes adjust to the dimly lit interior and the clanging of steel on steel told her that Jake was busy at the anvil. She walked towards the glow of the forge, "Howdy Jake!" she called, raising her voice to be heard above the ring of hammer on anvil. A big man that fit the image of a smithy, leather apron over a massive girth, hairy shoulders pushing out from the thin shirt, hobnail boots that supported his broad stance, but with a rosy nose and cheeks and a broad smile made friendly by a sparkle in his eyes as he turned to face Cora.

"Well, howdy girl! What brings you down here?"

Cora dropped her eyes, twisted her hands together, and said, "I need a wagon an' four mules!"

"What for? You goin' somewhere?"

"Yup, me'n the kids are headed to Californy!"

He lay the hammer on the anvil and leaned back, taking a long look at his friend, "Hear from that no-account husband of yours?"

She looked at him and started to tell about the letter she had received with the news about her husband, but she had kept that secret for so long, she couldn't let it out now. Not to Jake, he had been moonin' after her for over a year now and she had put him off by saying she was married. So, she decided to use that as a reason, "Yeah, sure did. He wants us to come and join him. Said he's got hisself a good claim and makin' good money. Sides, this ain't no place to raise kids, that Reuben's been gettin' himself into mischief again and he needs a man's hand to keep him in line. So, we're goin'. As to them mules, I want some that I can ride if'n I need to, and maybe a saddle horse to tag along as well. I want a good sturdy wagon, but not one o' them Conestoga, they're too big."

Jake looked at Cora, shook his head, and said, "Foller me."

CHAPTER FIVE
STRAY

TATE LEANED BACK IN HIS CHAIR ON THE PORCH, CROSSED HIS legs and held the newspaper out in front to catch the light. A copy of the Boston Evening Transcript, just over a month old, had been left behind by Alexander Barclay and this was the first day after his departure and Tate was anxious to catch up on the news. Maggie brought out two cups of coffee, handed one to Tate and kept the other for herself, seating herself in her rocker to enjoy the morning. The youngsters were playing in the clearing, Sean showing his usual protectiveness for his sister, as he ran interference between her and Lobo. The wolf was trying to get the bit of bacon that Sadie was chewing on but wouldn't do anything to hurt either of the children, and both the kids were laughing at the playful antics of the big ball of fur.

"Well, lookee here, just what we need, another political party! The U.S. Republican Party held its first meeting in Jackson, Michigan, and I bet they didn't get anything accomplished. Politicians!" he declared with a touch of disgust, but he kept reading. "Well, there is one thing I agree with 'em about, it 'pears they are anti-slavery! According to Lex, the nation is shaping up to a fight between the slavers and those agin' it. If it ain't one thing it's another, politicians always find somethin' to argue about." He popped the paper and turned the page, let it lie on his legs as he took a sip of coffee and looked up at the kids. "Looks like Lobo's showin' his age a little, not as fast as he used to be."

"Ummhumm, but he can still move when he needs to, you can bet on that," answered Maggie. "When you get through with that," motioning to the paper, "I want to look at the advertisements."

"Says here that last fall there was a cholera epidemic in London, killed 10,000 people. Some doctor there traced it to a water pump and he says it proves that cholera is water-borne. That means carried by the water," he explained.

"I know what waterborne means. They knew that after that epidemic in St. Louis!"

"And there was a couple ships that collided off the coast of Newfoundland, says here there were 320 killed. You'd think with all that ocean, they could keep from runnin' into each other." He laid the paper down and looked to Maggie, "See there, we ain't missin' nothin' important livin' in these mountains! Why, it's a whole lot safer for our younguns' here in the mountains than back east in all that stuff!"

"You won't get any argument from me!" She sipped her coffee and took it away from her mouth suddenly, pointed to Lobo, who was standing rigid, ears up and eyes narrowed, looking toward the trees.

Tate saw the move of the wolf and spoke to the young-sters, "Get up here on the porch, now!"

He reached for the ever-present Hawken, checked the load, and slipped the possibles bag and powder-horn over his head. Maggie herded the children into the house while Tate tiptoed off the porch to take up a position at the corner of the cabin. He immediately recognized the sound of approaching hoofbeats, coming toward the cabin at a trot, but was surprised to see a rider-less mule appear. The animal was obviously frightened, the pack-harness was hanging under his belly and dragging the ground, and as Tate approached, speaking softly and with an outstretched hand, the mule stopped and looked at the man with wide eyes and flared nostrils. He was nervously shaking but stretched out his nose to sniff the approaching man, and when Tate touched his head, the mule jerked back, but didn't move away. Within moments, Tate held the halter and dragging lead rope and was stroking the neck of the animal, calming it down. He looked back to the porch and called for Maggie to come near.

"Hold his lead rope while I get this pack saddle off him," he instructed.

"Is this one of Barclay's?" asked Maggie, remembering the mules led by the trader just the day before.

"I'm pretty sure he is, look at his haunch there. See those claw marks? That's grizzly."

"Oh no, you don't mean . . . "

"Yup, apparently the trader run into a grizz, mebbe even the one we saw," suggested Tate as he loosed the pack saddle from the animal. He took the lead rope from Maggie and led the mule into the corral. He leaned on the top rail and looked at her, "I'm gonna have to back-track that mule and see if I can find Lex. Can't leave him out there, no matter what's happened."

Maggie nodded at Tate, understanding, "I was also thinking, after the Ute did that attack on Fort Pueblo last Christmas, you don't think they would have done this?" She was thinking of what some had called the Fort Pueblo massacre that happened when a band of Ute and Jicarilla Apache attacked the Fort and killed everyone.

"No, that wasn't Two Eagles bunch that did that, and that's where Lex was headed. No, this was a grizz I'm sure."

He was soon mounted and ready to leave, with a "I'll be back soon's I can," and a snap of the fingers to Lobo, he was on the back-trail of the wayward mule. It was pushing noon-time when Shady did a stutter-step, head lifted and ears forward, that warned Tate of trouble ahead. Lobo was in the middle of the trail and he too had stopped, showing the signs of alarm. Tate stepped down, his new Sharps rifle in hand and the Colt Dragoon in the holster at his side. He reared the hammer back to set the front trigger, and started a stealthy approach through the trees, staying to the side of the trail with Lobo just before him.

There was a noise coming from the narrow clearing, he couldn't make it out, but Lobo dropped down, head lowered, and ears pinned back as his lip curled showing his fangs as he let a low growl rumble. "Easy boy, easy now," whispered Tate, taking each step slowly and quietly. When the trees parted to allow him to see into the clearing, he sucked air at the sight. The big sorrel that Lex rode was a bloody mess and the grizzly was making a meal out of the horse's innards. Behind the bear, an equally bloody mule was sprawled, his head and neck looking like it had been through a meat grinder. Tate could only see the booted leg of Lex just beyond the bear, unable to see the rest of the man, but the boot didn't move. The bear was ripping and tearing, growling all the while as if his vented anger made the feast more appetizing.

Whiskey Jacks, Ravens, and Magpies fought and squawked for scraps as one foolish coyote snatched at the remains of the mule. A turkey buzzard swooped down and caught the attention of the bear who whirled and swiped at the black bird to send it on its way. When he turned back to his feast, he caught a whiff of the wolf and looked up to see the grey beast in a crouch, ready to attack. Tate lifted the rifle to his shoulder as the grizzly rose to his full threatening height, but Lobo had one paw lifted, set it down, and lifted the other, slowly approaching and keeping the bear's attention. Tate drew in a breath, let it out slowly, and as he started to pull the trigger, the bear dropped to all fours to charge. Lobo leaped at the beast but was swatted aside as he was nothing more than a pesky nuisance.

Tate squeezed off the shot and saw a puff of dust at the bear's shoulder, saw the grizz stumble, but keep coming. Tate dropped the rifle and pulled the Colt, cocking it as he brought it up, took a quick aim at the bear's head, and fired. The bear flinched but didn't slow his charge. Tate fired again, again, again, and with the bear no more than ten or twelve feet away and barreling down, the big beast roared, and Tate saw teeth and tongue, aimed at the open mouth and fired again. The mouth closed and still he came, with the beast only a couple of paces away, Tate aimed at the bear's eye and fired his last shot. The bear's head turned, but the momentum of the charge kept him on course and he hit Tate full on and knocked him to the ground and the beast tumbled over the man.

Tate rolled, and scrambled to his feet as the now clumsy grizzly turned and roared, one-eyed, to raise up on his hind feet. He pawed at the air with his one good paw and leaned forward to come at the man. Tate snatched his big Bowie knife from the scabbard at his back and the two collided as the bear tried to take Tate's head in his mouth. Tate thrust the Bowie into the belly of the beast, ripping the razor-sharp blade up to open the guts of the grizz. The two seemed to dance together, with arms entwined, and then fell with Tate under the colossus. Dust rose as the bodies crashed to the ground and grunts came from both, but neither moved.

The birds had scattered, the coyote ran, and the woods were completely silent for just a moment. Lobo rose, padded toward the thick furred mountain of meanness that lay atop his master, and licked at the face of his friend. Tate's eyes fluttered, and he sucked air, as he looked around, seeing nothing but silver-tipped brown fur. He gasped and grunted, pushing at the burden and with considerable effort, finally managed to extricate himself from under the bear. He rubbed his right eye, brought away a bloody hand and set down on a log to examine his wounds. He felt a deep cut in his scalp and another just below his cheekbone, but the facial cut wasn't as bad. He stood and looked at the carnage of the animals, remembered Lex and staggered to where he had seen the booted leg. The bear had covered Lex with leaves, pine needles and anything else that lay around, planning on coming back to this tidbit after he gorged himself of horse-meat. Tate brushed away the debris from the man's head, saw several wounds from teeth and claw on the back of his head, neck and shoulders. As he cleared away more debris, he was startled to hear a moan come from the man. Tate quickly rolled him over and saw his eyes flutter and then the trader took a deep breath and mumbled something indiscernible.

"Take it easy, Lex. I'll get you outta here real soon. I'm gonna go get my horse and we'll get you back to the house and Maggie'll fix you up proper."

THE TRADER'S WALL TENT LOOKED A LITTLE OUT OF PLACE AT the tree line of the clearing. With the cabin set back against the cliff wall and the corrals extending to the side, the wall tent was across the clearing and looked very temporary compared to the rest of the structures. The front flap was thrown back as Tate exited, unable to stand to his full height until free from the shade flaps that stretched out above the entry. He looked around the clearing and started for the porch where Maggie sat, sewing on her newest project made from the wool plaid from the trader.

As Tate stepped up onto the porch, Maggie asked, "How's he doin'?"

"He still can't or won't sit up, hasn't eaten much, but he's sure liking that tea you fixed. What'd you make that with?"

"A recipe I got from White Flower, now that she's the medicine woman with the Comanche, she's quite the expert in the herbs and plants. That's a concoction made from the sticky red resin on the fresh buds of Aspen, and the inner bark of willow. That resin is what the old-timers called the Balm of Gilead."

"Ya don't say, why, I remember my ma talkin' 'bout the Balm of Gilead, but she was referring to the blood of Jesus, how it wipes away all sin."

"Well, this doesn't do anything for sin, but it is good for just about anything that ails a person." She looked down at the material in her lap and added, "That old man is mighty lucky to still be alive after what he's been through."

"Yes'm, he sure 'nuff is. If you'da seen what that grizzly did to that horse and mule, you wouldn'ta thot it possible that a man could survive such an attack."

"Well, that hide's going to make a mighty fine robe or whatever, that fur was thick. But he had a few scars on him too."

Tate grinned and nodded his head as he spoke, "A bear doesn't get that big and that old without getting into more'n his share of scrapes and fights. When I skinned him, I found every bullet I put in him, another fresh one, probably from Lex, and three others from old wounds. They were smaller caliber, probably from some trade rifles the Indians had or coulda been an older flinter from a mountain man long gone, or et mebbe."

"Ewww, you mean to tell me that bear might have eaten someone before?"

"Probably, that's why he wasn't scared of man's scent. He just thought it was the smell of dinner!" he chuckled as he watched Maggie's face contort with the thought.

"Well, I'm glad you didn't bring any bear meat back for us to eat. I don't think I could handle eating something that had made a meal of some other man." She focused her attention on her sewing, wanting to get the image out of her mind.

"Nah, bear meat in the Spring ain't much good. All their winter fat's been used up and they get pretty rank after they come outta hibernation. Now, in the fall, when they're all fattened up for winter, now that's the time when bear meat's good, yessir." He licked his lips for emphasis and closed his eyes, smiled and rubbed his belly.

"Pa, when we goin' bear huntin'?" asked Sean, bringing Tate's eyes suddenly open. Tate had been leaning back against the cabin wall, the front legs of the ladder-back chair off the floor but Sean's question brought him down.

"Why son, there's a lotta huntin' you need to experience before we go after any bear. Sides, you wouldn't wanna run onto Buster would'ja?"

"No, reckon not. I miss that bear, don't you?"

"Sometimes, but he got so big he was hard for you to handle. It's one thing to have a bear for a pet, but they don't stay too friendly after they grow up. If he rolled over on top of you he woulda squashed the livin' daylights outta you. Nah, he needed to find him a mate and become a daddy like all other bears do, you know, have a family."

"Yeah, an' I wouldn't wanna shoot one of his young'uns either," replied Sean, with a bit of a pooch-mouth pout.

Tate rubbed the boys head and said, "Since most of our chickens survived the winter, why don't you get your sister and go see if we got some eggs? Maybe we could get your ma to fix us up some eggs an' pork belly in the morning for breakfast."

They watched the two siblings trot off to the chicken shed that sat between the house and the tack shed, close to the entry to the cavern they used for cold storage of their meat and other goods. Sean carried the basket and Sadie ran ahead, anxious to find more eggs than her brother. Maggie looked to Tate and said, "They are growing so fast, it's hard to believe we've been here long enough for our son to be almost ten years old. Next thing we know, he'll be wanting to find himself a girlfriend somewhere. And what are we going to do then?"

"Uh, aren't you rushing things a bit? I mean, he's still a boy and you've practically got him married off!"

"Well, I think about things like that. With no one else around, what's he going to do, marry some Indian girl?"

"What would be wrong with that? There's plenty o' fine Ute and Comanche girls. Now, if he got a hankerin' fer one o' them Jicarilla Apache, well, I don't know about that, but . . . "

"Oh, you!" she pouted as she folded her arms across her chest.

He laughed and said, "I didn't have to go anywhere to find me a fine woman! Here I was mindin' my own business and 'fore I knew it, this wild woman from Ireland came trompin' into my life and look at me now! All married and kids and a home, ain't it amazing what God can do when we just get out of His way?"

She had tried to keep a mad on, but a slow smile split her face and she slapped playfully at his arm and started to giggle. "Oh you, you're right. God knows what He's doing, and I should just let things be since I can't change 'em anyway."

"What say we go check on our patient?" asked Tate, standing and holding out a hand to help Maggie to her feet.

Tate entered the tent first, motioned for Maggie to follow, and the two knelt down beside the injured man, prostrate on the buffalo robe. They knew the man would prefer his privacy in his tent, to being stepped around in the middle of the cabin floor, and Maggie knew the smells of the poultices and such would be a bit fragrant for the close confines.

"I brought your favorite nurse for ya' Lex," said Tate as Maggie pulled the blanket back from the trader's torso. He was lying on his stomach with his head turned toward his visitors and simply grunted to acknowledge them.

Maggie slowly removed the poultices and set them aside, looking at each of the wounds, the worst being on his shoulders where the grizz had dug his claws in deep and ripped them across this back. Maggie had sewn the worst of the gashes together, using fine twisted sinew, and now examined her handiwork. She was looking for any inflammation or bleeding and was pleased to see the wounds were healing. She moved the container with the poultice blend closer and applied fresh ones to the wounds before covering them with a clean cloth. With Lex unable to rise, she could only hold the bandages on with the weight of the blanket. Satisfied with her ministrations, she leaned back and said, "It's only been four days Lex, but you're starting to heal up just fine. If you move around too much, those bandages will come off, so try to limit your movements."

He grunted to acknowledge her instructions, muttered a whispered "Thanks Maggie," and closed his eyes, sighing in relief.

She finished tending the wounds in his hair, nodded to Tate and stood to leave. "If you can take any more of that tea, drink as much as you can. It'll help with the pain." He grunted again as she exited the tent. Tate followed her out and she turned to him, "I've got his buckskins, what's left of them, soaking in the tub out back. The blood'll come out alright, but I'm not sure his top is going to be salvageable. He might need a new top or something." She looked at Tate, cocked her head to the side, "Say, that old shirt you got tore up when you had that set-to with the lion, maybe I can use what's left of that and the rags of Lex's and make a passable shirt out of the two. Yeah, that's what I'll do, that is if you don't mind, husband." She smiled up at her man to entice his approval.

"Oh, I s'pose so, tain't good for nuthin' like it is, so go 'head on." He feigned hurt, but Maggie knew he was even more generous than she had ever been. "So, how long do you think it'll be 'fore he can get up and around a bit?"

"I don't want him moving around too much, don't want him to split open those wounds. But, I think another four or five days and he'll be mended enough where he can at least sit up, if not get up and move around. He'll need to start eating better, but that's going to take one of us feeding him since he's lying on his belly."

"I never thought I'd see the day that old man didn't have an appetite."

"Oh, I think he'll get his appetite back soon enough. Then you'll probably have to go find another elk just to keep him fed!" explained Maggie as she started back to the cabin. She needed to gather some more plants for her poultices and most of them grew down in the creek bottom. After the trader's experience, she wasn't about to go alone, "So, you get the horses ready, and I'll get us something to eat, and we'll go to the creek to get some more plants and give the kids a change of scenery."

Tate grinned and swatted at Maggie's rump, but she swished away and shook her finger at him as he turned to the corrals. He turned back to her and hollered, "Hey, that'll give us a chance to get in a little shootin' with our new pistols an' such!" Although he had already 'practiced' with both his Sharps and Colt on the grizz, he wanted Maggie to get comfortable with using her Baby Dragoon and maybe try his Sharps. She waved at him from the porch and disappeared inside.

CHAPTER SEVEN
WAGONS

THEY WERE SIX DAYS OUT OF KANSAS CITY, FORMERLY KNOWN as Westport, the town that had become the supply and shipping point for William Bent of Bent's Fort. It was there that Cora and her family had joined with five other wagons that had signed on with William Bent to travel the Sante Fe Trail from Missouri to his trading fort on the Arkansas River. It was in the newly named Kansas Territory, although Bent still called it 'the territories.' After getting outfitted in St. Joseph, the four days travel to Kansas City was what Cora called their 'shakedown cruise' to get used to handling the wagon and mules.

The twins, Reuben and Rachel, were still excited that they were going to California and would be joining the gold rush. Reuben was the one full of questions, "Ma, do you think Pa really struck it rich?"

She turned her head to look directly at the boy, standing behind the seat in the box of the wagon, "Your pa's idea of striking it rich and mine, are two different things. If he hit a good jackpot at the Faro table, he'd say he 'struck it rich', but my idea would be to get enough to last the rest of your life, an' never havin' to work again." She slapped the mules on their rumps to keep up the pace. The back pair had a tendency to get a little lazy and seemed to doze off, making the whip necessary to keep their attention.

"You did say he had a good claim and was doing good, didn'tcha?" queried the boy, anxious for any and all details about his absentee father.

"The last I heard from him, that's what he said. Now, how 'bout you climb up here an' take these reins. 'Bout time you started earnin' your keep." She handed the reins to the boy and the two swapped places, leaving Rachel still on the seat beside him. Cora was still struggling with telling the twins that their father was dead, died in a shooting over a poker table. Yet she was still faced with the truth that there was no one waiting for them in the goldfields. She stood behind the twins, one hand on each shoulder, and she resigned herself to her task. She turned back to the trunk with her belongings, opened it, and dug around until she found the letter. When she straightened up and turned back to the twins, she saw the buildings in the distance that Bent told her would be their stopping place for the night. The town, if it could be called that, of Council Grove, sat on the edge of the Kaw Indian reservation. She drew a deep breath, "Kids, there's somethin' I have to tell ya."

Both turned to look at their mother, recognizing the tone of her voice that said either they were in trouble, or there was something serious about to be said.

"What is it, Ma?" asked Rachel, the quiet one, with a concerned and fearful expression.

"I got this letter a while back and I couldn't bring myself to tell you 'bout it. Just listen while I read, 'Mrs. Ritter, your man, Luther, was a friend an' asked me to write'chu this here letter. He was kilt today when he caught a cheat at poker. They hung him, the one whut cheated. Luther didn't have much after the digger was done. But here 'tis. $2.50. Sorry. Rufus Jessup.'"

"You m-m-mean Pa's dead?" stuttered Reuben.

"When did he die?" asked Rachel, just above a whisper.

"I don't rightly know. There ain't no date on the letter, but I got it a while back. I just couldn't tell ya, that's all."

"Well, then, why're we goin' to California?" demanded Reuben, starting to pull back on the reins to stop the wagon.

"Don't stop, there's wagon's behind us!" ordered Rachel.

He let up on the reins and the mules resumed their pace. "Why, Ma?" asked Reuben again.

She wanted to say, 'to keep you outta jail!' but she said, "We needed us a new start. St. Joe was just not a good place for you young'uns."

"But why all the way to California? Are you thinking about prospecting for gold?" asked Rachel, unbelieving.

"Well, we might not go all the way to California, not if we find someplace sooner. Let's just call it an adventure, you know, like them explorers you're always talkin' 'bout."

It was no surprise to Cora that the twins showed little remorse for the loss of their father. He had been absent for most of their lives, and even when present he showed little concern and even less affection for any member of his family. His itchy feet and constant chase of the wandering star often put him in melancholy moods where he was unreachable by those nearby. He was a stranger to the twins for most of their lives and the only real image they had of their father was one they had imagined.

A meaningful glance passed between the twins, reflecting that uncommon bond and communication known only by close siblings. They had often shared thoughts about their impulsive and idiosyncratic, mother. But they had been raised to expect anything at any time, with a father that had a bad case of wanderlust and a mother with a sense of adventure, anything could happen and quite often did. They simultaneously drew deep breaths and dropped their shoulders in resignation.

Council Grove had all of three buildings, an untended livery, a trading post, and a building that sat opposite the others and had a sign, "Agent." They were soon to find that the trading post had been established to do business with the Kaw Indians on the reservation, and the building marked "Agent," was the office of the Indian Agent that was most often empty. The trader had living quarters in back of his post and the agent used his office space for his sleeping quarters as well. The buildings sat on the east bank of the Neosho River and the freight wagons passed them by without slowing. When all the wagons were across the river, they circled up for the night and cookfires made with buffalo chips were soon smoking and blazing.

William Bent had a habit of stopping by all the fires and checking on everyone before he turned in, and as he stopped by the Ritter fire, Reuben was quick to ask, "Mr. Bent, I thought this was where an Indian reservation was, but I don't see any Indians. How come?"

Bent propped a foot on the stool by the fire and chuckled before he said, "These are the Kaw Indians, they're a peaceful people, used to be a part of the Osage. I said they're peaceful, and that's true, they are with the whites, but not with the Kiowa and Comanche or even the Pawnee. This is their reservation, it's not as big as it used to be, but it's still pretty sizeable and you'll see their main village tomorrow. They'll probably be leaving the village soon to go on their buffalo hunt, a little farther west of here."

"Do we have any reason to be concerned?" asked a rather timid Rachel.

"No, not at all. Like I said, they're peaceable. Not like some of the other tribes. There are those we might run into farther along that aren't quite so easy to get along with."

"You mean we might get in an Injun fight?" Reuben asked excitedly.

"It's possible. But trust me, there's nothing about an 'Injun fight,' as you call it, that is appealing in any way."

"What tribe of Injuns might we have to fight?"

"Well, I've dealt with all the different tribes and I hope we can pass through peacefully. But, if there's any bunch that might not be too friendly, it's the Kiowa. They're a fierce people and haven't been treated too well by whites, especially after the Indian Removal Act of 1830 that moved a lot of different native peoples from their homelands. All of the tribes of the plains know about the Trail of Tears and all are concerned that might happen to them."

"The Trail of Tears? Never heard of it," stated Reuben.

"That happened in 1838 when the government marched 16,000 native peoples from their homelands in the east to what they called Indian Territory, south of here. That was over 1,200 miles and more than a quarter of them died."

"A quarter, that's over 4,000!" declared Rachel, astounded. "Why didn't we know about that?"

"Well, that's not something the government likes to talk about," answered Bent, dropping his foot from the stool and turning to leave.

"Mr. Bent, you sound, well, sympathetic for the Indian, why?" asked Cora.

"I am a member of the Cheyenne tribe. I am a sub-chief of the people, I have an Indian wife, and I have five children that are part Cheyenne. As a matter of fact, when I left my home in the west, I brought my son, George, or as he is called in Cheyenne, *Ho-my-ike,* with me and enrolled him in the Episcopal boarding school in Kansas City."

"Oh," was all Cora could say, as she dropped her eyes to the fire.

William Bent, touched the brim of his hat, "You folks enjoy your evening," and departed.

CHAPTER EIGHT
HUNT

"So, how ya' doin' this mornin', Lex?" asked Tate as he pushed aside the entry flap of the wall tent. He was surprised to see Lex sitting up in the willow branch chair. It was Tate's first try at fashioning a piece of furniture and it had turned out right comfortable. Lex patted the arms of the chair to show his approval as it now held the lean frame of the trader.

Alexander Barclay patted his palms on the braided arms of the chair and answered, "I do believe I'm gonna survive. If I'da knowed how comfortable this here chair was, I mighta got outta them robes and into it a mite sooner. You done a mighty fine job o' this." He nodded his head to emphasize the point and in doing so, the new part in his hair showed the pink of the healing gouge from the teeth of the grizzly. He sat without a shirt over his torso, showing the strips of bandaging that held the poultices in place. His buckskin britches, newly scrubbed and repaired by Maggie, covered his bottom half. The fringe on the pants legs dangled from his crossed legs and barely covered his familiar moccasins.

"Wal, it's been goin' on two weeks since your little midnight dance with the grizzly and I was beginnin' to think you was just hangin' around because you like Maggie's cookin'."

"By jove, her cookin's good'nuff to make any man wanna hang around, but, believe you me, if'n I coulda got outta them covers any sooner, I'da dunnit," declared the trader, his tobacco stained beard bouncing on his chest with every syllable.

Tate chuckled as he dropped to the pile of blankets and buffalo robe and looked at the man, "You're lookin' a mite better this mornin', course those bandages and poultices are needin' changed, and I reckon you've got your appetite back. Maggie thinks it'll take another couple weeks 'fore you're able to sit a horse or do anything of the sort. What'chu think?"

"I think your woman's right. It do feel good to sit in this hyar chair, but that grizz didn't only lay me open with them claws an' teeth of his, he squeezed me might tight an' broke a few ribs too. Ever' time I suck wind, it feels like he's squeezin' me again."

"You never did tell me 'bout that little set to, just what happened anyway?"

"That darned thing snuck up on us from downwind, he was practically on us 'fore e'en the horse an' mules heard or smelt him! He stood up and darn near slapped the head off'n the horse, and I was fightin' my covers an' grabbin' fer my Sharps when he turned on me! I barely got off one shot when he slapped that rifle plum outta my hands an' the next thing I know, he was on top o me and playin' mumbly peg on muh ribs. Onliest thing I could do was play dead, which didn't take a lot a pretendin' cuz fer a while there, I thought I was already on the glory road to Heaven! Next thing I remember, I looked up an saw yore ugly face an' thought fer shore that grizzly had a little brother!"

Tate laughed at the expressions of the old man and

replied, "I went back an' got what stuff of your'n I could find, only one of your mules came back and the pack was hangin' 'round his belly. But whatever was in those packs is probably spread all over these mountains, but as you can tell," and he looked around the tent, motioning to the stuff stacked in the corners, "I fetched back what I could."

"The onliest reason that mule still had his packsaddle on is cuz with that'n, I just loosen the rigs an' leave it on him. He plays hob ever' time I need to put the packs on, so, he just keeps 'em. But, I'm beginnin' ta think I need to find me some better way to make a livin'." He paused for a moment, thoughtful, and asked, "Didja ever think 'bout that Californy? You know, the gold rush an' all. I heard tell they was pickin' up nuggets right off the ground."

"Now, Lex, you know that can't be true. But, with all the folks that're goin' there, I reckon a young enterprisin' sort such as you could find a way to make a livin' without havin' to go diggin' for it." Tate stood to leave the tent, and looked at the man seated before him, "Maggie'll be in after a bit to change your bandages, but me'n the boy are gonna be gone fer a couple days on a short meat hunt. This'll be the first time just me'n him go, so Maggie'll take good care of you while I'm gone."

The trader waved his hand and nodded his head, "Good luck on your hunt!" Tate returned the nod and exited the tent. It was early yet, and the sun had yet to clear the mountains behind the cabin and the shadows of the pines stretched across the clearing. Sean was at the corral, saddling his horse, excited about the coming hunt. As Tate neared, he saw the boy had already brought their bedrolls and saddle-bags from the house and stacked them beside the pole fence.

Tate leaned on the top rail and watched the boy pull on the latigo to tighten the girth, and with the leather strap over his shoulder, he kneed the steel dust stallion in the ribs to get him to let out his air, so the boy could tighten the cinch. When he wrapped the latigo over, around, and under, he slipped it through the wrap and pulled it tight, slipping the end in the loop beneath the pommel. Tate smiled at the work of his son, nodded his approval and said, "I'll go get the rest of our gear, you put the bridle on Shady and I'll be right back."

"Alright, Pa. I'll do it."

When Tate returned, he had the rifle scabbards with the Sharps in one and a Hawken in the other. Both bows had their own sheaths and Tate lay them atop the stacks beside the quivers of arrows. This was to be a hunt with the bows, but it was always smart to have heavier firepower along, just in case. Maggie came from the house, parfleche in her arms, to give her men an official send-off. The rawhide container held the essential things for the camp; coffee pot, frying pan, coffee, and best of all, the food. She had put in some biscuits, cornbread, pemmican, potatoes, beans, and a nice elk roast. Since they were only going to be gone for two days, that would be more than ample for the two hungry hunters.

With everything ready, Maggie gave Sean a big hug, kissed his cheek, and said, "You take good care of your pa, now, y'hear?"

Sean smiled broadly and answered, "Oh, I will, Ma. I'll take good care of him!"

The embrace between husband and wife embarrassed Sean and he turned away with a "Eewww" but Tate just squeezed Maggie a little tighter and after kissing her again, he looked down at her green eyes and said, "We'll be goin' up above Zapata falls. It's good country and the boy'll have a chance at just 'bout anything. But, we'll be back tomorrow evenin', maybe even after dark."

"You be sure you do and be sure to bring us some fresh meat. That ol' man in there," nodding her head toward the wall tent, "will be eating up everything that holds still long enough for him to sink his teeth into. Once he got his appetite back, he's making up for lost time."

Tate chuckled as he climbed aboard Shady, bent to grab the lead rope of the pack-mule and reined around to lead the way from the clearing. They dropped below the tree line and started on the trail that took the narrow strip between the trees and the dunes, as they headed south along the Sangre de Cristo mountain range. Once clear of the dunes, they rode along the shoulder that held bunch grass, sage, cactus and scattered piñons. As Tate looked at the land, his eyes roved from the tree line to his left and the drop off of the shoulder about two hundred yards to his right. This was flat country that afforded little cover, so the riders stayed close to the skirt of green that fell from the timberline high up on the Sangres.

It was late afternoon when Tate pointed Shady to a trail that mounted a ridge south of Zapata creek. Lobo eagerly took to the trail, liking the forested slopes better than the wide-open flats. Tate pulled to the side of the trail and waited for Sean to come alongside. "Son, the trail here leads on up this ridge and follows the creek down in the bottom. Right about here," pointing to the narrow gorge below them, "is where the falls are, and then farther up it opens into a nice little valley. Now, we're gonna take it easy, Lobo's up front there, and we might even jump some game before we make camp. So, you step on down and string your bow and slip the quiver over your shoulder."

Sean smiled broadly, eagerly slipping to the ground and taking his new bow from the sheath under the saddle fender. The quiver hung from the saddle horn and he waited till he was back aboard before slipping it over his shoulder and neck, to hang at his back. "I'm ready Pa!" he declared eagerly.

"Alright. But, we'll be ridin' quiet now, and if I motion like this," he held his hand flat, palm down, "you stop and don't ask questions. If I think you can get a shot, or need to do a bit of a stalk, I'll motion you. Understand?"

"Sure Pa, I understand."

Tate looked up the trail and saw Lobo, frozen in a half-stance, one foot lifted and ears forward, lip curling. Tate turned to the boy, motioning for him to step down. Once to the ground, Tate led his horse and pack-mule into the thicker trees, with Sean following close behind. Once they were well hidden, Tate whispered, "Lobo's onto something. You stay here with the horses, I'll go check it out. It might be Indians, so be ready with both your Hawken and an arrow!" He turned away from the boy and disappeared into the trees toward the trail.

When the wolf sensed Tate to be near, he backed away from the trail, and trotted into the trees to be beside the man. Tate dropped to one knee as Lobo neared and spoke to the wolf, "What'd you see, boy?" A low snarling growl told Tate it wasn't meat on the hoof that had alarmed the wolf. He leaned close beside the low branches of a spruce and watched the trail. The path they had followed had been hard packed and would show little sign of their passing, but an alert tracker would easily tell the trail had been disturbed, if by nothing else than fresh stirred pine needles.

Within moments, Tate heard the approach of horses and he dropped a hand to the scruff of Lobo, whispering, "I know, easy now." As he watched, several riders cleared the timber into the slight opening along the trail. Five Jicarilla Apache warriors, two with rifles and the others with bows and lances. They were watching the trees and were leading two horses with the butchered carcasses of elk. *A hunting party, maybe they won't be looking for trouble,* thought Tate as he watched them draw closer. They were almost past when the snap of a twig broke the silence of the forest. Tate whirled around to see Sean walking towards him and he motioned for the boy to stop where he was. Tate looked back to see the Apache had reined up and were looking into the trees. He was certain they could not see the boy, but if any other sound came, they would search it out. They waited, looking, moving only their eyes, to watch the passing Indians. The horses were absolutely still, having been trained well by their riders. Tate's breath came with shallow gasps, his hand on Lobo's neck to keep him from attacking.

As if on cue, everyone relaxed, and the Apache gigged their horses forward, little being said, but enough so that Tate knew they had not been detected. When the sound of the horses on the trail diminished and Tate judged the Indians to be well on their way, he turned and motioned for Sean to join him and Lobo. He stood as the boy approached and asked, "Why didn't you stay with the horses like I said?"

"I didn't want to miss out on getting an elk or a deer," explained the boy, obviously still excited about the hunt.

"Did you see what you missed?"

"No, what was it?"

"A hunting party of Jicarilla Apache, and if they had seen us, our scalps would probably be hanging from their lances and your mother wouldn't be too happy!"

"Apache?" the boy almost whispered as he looked to the trail expecting to see attacking Indians.

"Yes, Apache. Now, maybe you'll understand how important it is for you to do exactly what I say. Do you think you can do that now?"

Sean dropped his head to his chest and his arms hung to his side, the new longbow touching the ground as his shame filled him. "Yes Pa, I can. I'm sorry."

"Alright then, let's go get the horses and go on to the park and maybe find us some game. We'll probably not see anything until after we make camp, what with that hunting party passing through. They did have 'em a couple elk on their pack animals though, so maybe there's a herd up there waitin' for us."

The boy looked up at his father, hopeful of both his forgiveness and for a good hunt. He had long dreamed of this hunt and he wanted to show his father he was man enough to do the job. If only he could get an elk, then his Pa would know for sure! It was the same thought that filled the minds of the younger generation of boys and men since the beginning of time, a son wanting to be like his father and become a man.

CHAPTER NINE
KIOWA

CORA AND REUBEN WERE MORE INTERESTED IN THE KAW village than was Rachel. She was more concerned with a young man in one of the wagons that trailed behind theirs. His family was also bound for California and he was an only child, about 14, and his curly blonde hair and freckle face caught Rachel's attention. While she was busy talking to the young Michael Garmin, who rode alongside their wagon on his buckskin horse, Cora and Reuben were eyeballing the Indian village.

"Those sure are strange lodges they live in," commented Reuben as he pointed to the long lodges, "they look like giant worms that crawled up on top o' the ground, what with them round tops an' such. Mr. Bent said the main lodge is 'bout 60 feet by 25 feet. But lots of 'em are round. He says they look like that cuz they're covered with tree bark and hides and such. But he also said that when they go on a buffalo hunt, they use tipis like other plains tribes." Reuben was standing behind his mother who was busy with the leads to the mules. One of the bullwhackers had given her what he called a buggy whip, a long flexible rawhide covered pole with a braided leather quirt at the end. She had learned to make the whip crack like a small caliber pistol shot and the mules had responded well.

"I'm glad you're learnin' a lot from Mr. Bent but I'd like it better if'n you paid more attention to your readin' and 'rithmetic. They'll do you more good than knowin' 'bout a bunch o' Indians out here in the middle o' nowhere."

IT HAD BEEN an uneventful almost nine days since they left Council Grove, apart from the occasional breakdown, runaway mules, and shortage of firewood that had to be replaced by buffalo chips. Reuben had stepped up and when he wasn't driving the wagon, he was aboard their blaze faced bay mare they called Ruby, and riding with William Bent on point. Reuben was soaking up everything Bent shared and William was enjoying having an eager student to teach about the west.

With dusk approaching, Bent pointed out, "The river there, that's the Arkansas, and we'll be followin' it all the way to the Fort. This right here," and he pointed to the wide bend of the river, "is where the river changes directions and heads to the southeast. But we'll be stoppin' up yonder at Pawnee Rock." He pointed to a rise in the terrain about a half mile distant, that looked like a flat-top bald and low mesa surrounded by trees that covered the area from the rock to the river.

"Pawnee Rock? How come it's called that?"

Bent chuckled and looked at the boy, "There's two stories about that. One is that the Pawnee Indians, they mostly live up north o' here, used that as a council grounds, where the chiefs of the different tribes would meet and decide upon what they were going to do each year. But the other story is the one I like to think is where it got its name. It seems that several years back when a young Kit Carson, he was only bout seventeen at the time, was travelin' with a wagon train, an' it was his turn to stand guard. Well, he dozed off a little, and was startled awake by a noise an' he jumped up a shootin' thinkin' the Pawnee were attackin'. Come to find out he shot his own mule! Well, the rest o' the folks that was with him had a good laugh and they called it Pawnee Rock after that little incident. And the name stuck!"

Reuben looked at the man, trying to decide if he was spoofing or telling it true, and asked, "Is that true, did that really happen like that?"

"Ya know, I asked Kit about it once and he just laughed. Didn't deny it but didn't admit to it neither."

"You know Kit Carson? I read about him in one o' them penny novels."

"Know him? Why he's a good friend, comes to the Fort quite often, works for me some, too."

Bent turned his attention to the wagons and gave the motion to circle up near the small butte. They would be near the water and have a little protection from the wind with the butte at their back and it would be an easily defended site for their camp. With the freight wagons in the lead, the experienced teamsters started to form the circle as the covered wagons of the settlers and gold seekers followed in behind. As each wagon stopped with the team pointed away from the circle, everyone started unhitching the mules as several men were assigned to take the livestock down to the river to water and graze nearby.

Bent and Reuben rode up the slope to the top of the butte to look at the surrounding country and had just pulled rein as Bent stood in his stirrups to look at the wagons below. Reuben scanned the countryside, amazed at how far he could see. He turned in his saddle to look in the direction they had been traveling and saw movement. He thought it was some buffalo or other game and looked a little closer, "Uh, Mr. Bent," he started.

"Just a minute, Reuben, I want to watch the boys get the wagons sit . . . "

"Mr. Bent," demanded Reuben a little louder and stood in his stirrups to point where he saw the movement.

"What!" responded Bent angrily. He turned and saw the boy pointing, turned to see what he was so concerned about, and immediately shouted to the wagons below, "INDIANS!! Get your rifles!" and reined his horse around with a, "Come on, boy!" to Reuben and the two rode from the butte and back to the wagons.

By the time Reuben came to their wagon, Cora and Rachel had already drawn out their Sharps rifles and Reuben snatched his Hawken from the scabbard as he dropped to the ground. He checked to be certain of his load and the cap on the nipple as he eared back the hammer, and readied himself for the onslaught. Rachel and Cora lifted the canvas bonnet at the side of the wagon to provide enough space to shoot, seated themselves upon the boxes and trunks in the wagon, rested their big Sharps on the edge of the wagon box and set the triggers by pulling back the hammers, ready for the attack. Reuben preferred the Hawken and had perfected his reloading of the percussion cap rifle, so he could get at least three shots per minute, if he rushed it. But the women were using the paper cartridges and could get in as many as six, sometimes more, shots per minute. Cora, as a gunsmith, found it necessary to be proficient with any and all firearms and had taught her children as well, and now that would be put to the test.

Bent was surprised by the attack as he had traded with the Kiowa and knew many of their leaders, but what he didn't know was the tribe had been decimated by a smallpox epidemic and were bent on getting their revenge upon any and all whites. It was unusual for them to attack a wagon train the size of this one, with twenty-two freight wagons, ten bound for Bent's and the other twelve for Sante Fe, and the five covered wagons, this was a well-equipped and armed wagon train and the Indians would most often bypass one this large. But it was an angry and blood-thirsty war party that was riding down on this train.

"Hold your fire until you can make it count!" shouted William Bent, repeating himself in the other direction to make sure everyone heard. The mules that were yet to be unhitched were prancing nervously with all the action around them as the people threw down trunks, boxes, and bales to give cover. Some of the men were struggling to unhitch them before the Indians were too close, but most gave up and dove for cover.

"Wait till the others start shootin' girl," instructed Cora to Rachel. She knew Reuben would wait, but since she and Rachel had the only Sharps on the entire train, she didn't want to start the ball quite yet. The Sharps were a rare commodity in the west, but one in great demand, and that increased the cost beyond what most were able to afford. With an effective range of 1000 yards, the weapons had already become known by the few Indians that had seen them as the "Shoot today, kill tomorrow" rifle.

And suddenly the Kiowa were storming around the circle, rifles sounded amidst the screams and war cries of the attackers, several mules brayed as they became the target of the arrows and lances of the warriors. The blasts from the many rifles that fired in all directions sent a circle of grey smoke that settled around the wagons, masking the view of the attackers and defenders as well. Black powder smoke did not disperse quickly, but the fighting continued with nervous teamsters firing blindly at the war cries of the Kiowa.

Suddenly two warriors appeared out of the smoke before the Ritter wagon as Reuben had rolled to his side to reload his Hawken. But the two women fired their big Sharps almost simultaneously and the Indians were blasted from their horses as if they had been jerked back with a rope. The horses cut sharply to the side to avoid collision with the wagon and high-tailed it away from the melee. Reuben had just set the cap on the nipple and brought back the hammer when he saw a crouched Indian, trying to sneak through the smoke to attack. He swung the rifle to face the warrior as he charged holding his lance before him with both hands. But the blast from the Hawken sent the bullet through the man's chest and broke his backbone as it knocked the warrior to his back to lie unmoving.

The firing had abated, and the screaming ended as the attackers pulled back from the circle of wagons to regroup. William Bent trotted around the inside of the wagon circle, checking on everyone and saw Reuben underneath, but didn't see the women inside the wagon. He kicked the boy's foot and asked, "You alright there, Reuben?"

"Yeah, I'm fine."

"Where's the womenfolk?"

A voice came from within the wagon, "We're in here!"

He lifted the edge of the wagon's canvas bonnet and said, "Well, you ladies stay there. You'll be as safe there as . . . " but he stopped as both women turned to face him, and he saw they held Sharps rifles and their faces showed some powder residue from shooting. He looked from one to the other and said, "Oh, I didn't know. Say, are you shootin' Sharps?"

"Uhhnhuh," answered Cora, rolling her eyes at the remark.

"Can you hit anything with 'em?"

Cora just jerked her thumb over her shoulder for the man to look at the evidence beyond their wagon. He walked around the front and looked to see several slain Indians beyond. "Well, I'll be a monkey's uncle," he muttered as he looked from the Indians to the women. He shook his head as he walked away, mumbling to himself, and watched by Cora and Rachel who looked at one another and laughed.

When Bent returned to his central spot of command, he stood atop a box and hollered, "They'll probably be back in just a couple minutes, soon's the smoke rises an' they can see. Pick your targets and don't waste your powder. We might need all we got."

Everyone returned to their positions, adjusting whatever they had used for cover, situating themselves for better shooting positions, and watched for any movement. The Ritter wagon was just to the right of center of the line of wagons that faced the principal point of attack, and as the smoke cleared, Cora searched the distant flats for the gathering Indians. They had bunched up far enough away to be out of rifle range, or so they thought, and were readying themselves for another attack. Cora squinted her eyes, searching the group for any giveaway, and when she saw what she believed to be the leader, she spoke to Rachel. "See that'n kinda in the center, he's on a white horse and wavin' that lance in the air?"

"Yeah, what about him?"

"I think that's the leader. Let's both take aim, that's about 800 yards, so hold just over his head, and when I say now, we'll both shoot."

Rachel squirmed around a little, getting a more comfortable position and steadied the rifle. She eared back the hammer, setting the front trigger and brought the front blade sight in line with the buckhorn rear sight, said, "Anytime, Ma." She drew in a breath and let it part way out, held her finger on the trigger and waited.

Cora copied the action of her daughter and when she heard Rachel's breath escape, she whispered, "Now!"

Both rifles roared and bucked, stabbing the dwindling light with lances of smoke and fire, kicking both women back a couple of inches. Both raised their heads to look at their target and suddenly the man with the lance was knocked from his horse and the horse dropped to the ground. The warriors that had gathered around their chief, suddenly pulled back, some of the horses rearing up and screams and shouts echoed off the butte behind the wagons. The war party milled in confusion and quickly drew back to escape from any more rifle shots. Their confusion and fear showed as they kept looking back to the wagons, as if expecting judgment to rain down upon them with more long-distance bullets coming their way.

The people of the wagons were silent with shock and then all began talking at once. It was easy to make out, "Who made that shot? Where'd it come from?" A grinning and laughing Reuben slid from under the wagon and lifted the canvas to look at his ma and sister. "That was some shootin'! Which one hit the Indian and which one killed his horse?"

Cora and Rachel rolled to their sides, facing each other and looking at Reuben. Cora said, "Now how we s'posed to know that? We shot at the same time and hit 'bout the same place."

It didn't take William Bent long to realize where the shot came from and he walked back to the Ritter wagon, continually eyeing the Indians on the far rise. He saw Reuben talking to his mother and said, "Thank you ladies, or lady, whichever one of you made that shot. I think you saved us all a lot of grief."

"That's the way it is with the Ritter women, they're both mighty fine shots!" declared Reuben with pride.

But when Bent told his teamsters that a woman had saved

their bacon, they had a hard time swallowing what he said, as did the gold seekers and settlers. But all were glad she was on their side. And when they pulled out the next morning, the Ritter wagon was given the honor of being first in line, and it was surprising how mannerly all the teamsters were after that.

CHAPTER TEN
WAPITI

THEY CROSSED SOUTH ZAPATA CREEK TO REACH THE NORTH slope of California Gulch and made camp in a small grove of aspen. There was a lot of sign of elk, or wapiti as the natives called them, and Tate was hopeful for an opportunity for the boy to take his first elk with his bow. As they left their camp, the sun was cradled in the distant San Juans, launching its lances of gold and orange in every direction to make the mountains a silhouette before a glorious display of light. It was an ideal time for a hunt, the preferred time for animals to come from the thick timber into the valley bottom for both graze and water.

With their camp on the north slope of the wide draw of the California Gulch, they walked back toward Zapata Creek and planned to follow it upstream to the last fork of the two feeder creeks. They were just below timberline, but the valley provided excellent graze between the grassy creek bottom and the low growing tundra. They passed a few patches of blue-bells and the purple alpine forget-me-nots, and along the ridges were some of the bristlecone pines with their branches facing away from the prevailing winds and

the bark showing red windburn. Elk prefer the higher eleva-
tions during the summer months and secluded valleys like
the Zapata Creek gave all they needed.

Tate used hand signals to direct Sean along the trail that
kept them above the creek bottom and offered the cover of
scrub oak brush that he hoped would enable them to
approach any game. Lobo followed behind Sean and in front
of Tate, not happy with the doing, but obeying his friend's
commands. Suddenly, Sean stopped and froze in a slight
crouch, motioning to his dad to the tree line. Tiptoeing from
the trees was a young cow elk, followed by two more, a spike
bull, a new calf pushed along by his mother, and within
about six or seven yards, the velvet covered antlers of a bull
showed in the new green of the aspen. Tate moved up beside
his son and whispered, "Your best bet is that first bull, the
one with spikes even though they're not very long at this
stage, that way you won't take a cow that's yet to calve."

The boy nodded his understanding and looked to his
father for direction. "They're too far for a shot, ain't they?"
asked Sean, concerned.

"Yeah," responded Tate as he looked around for an
approach they might use to start a stalk of the animals. He
motioned to Sean to follow him as they turned back on the
trail. After backtracking about twenty yards, Tate pointed,
"Drop down on all fours and we'll crawl behind that low rise
yonder, that'll take us down to the willows and the creek. We
can cross over and come up in that bend and maybe you'll get
a shot from there."

Sean smiled and did as instructed, leading the way to the
willows. Lobo even dropped to his belly and crawled behind
the boy, although he could have walked without being seen
due to the slight knoll they were behind. Once to the
willows, Sean waded across the creek, followed by Lobo and
his dad, and at his dad's motioned instructions, dropped to a

crouch and moved upstream toward the elk that were over a hundred yards distant. After about sixty yards, his impatience got the better of him and he stood, pushed aside some willows, and sought to see the elk. The big cow in the front of the small herd snapped her head up, ears forward, and looked directly at the brush that moved. Tate had often told his son that it is movement that catches the eye of an observer, man or beast, and if he thought he might be in danger of being seen, to freeze. Even though he could be standing in plain sight, he would never know what background imagery could cause him to blend in and as long as he did not move, he could possibly go unseen. Fortunately, Sean remembered his dad's advice and froze, dropping his eyes from the elk, and waited. When his father whispered, "Now!" he slowly let the branch slide back into place and dropped his head from view.

"That was close, I just had to see where they were," came the vain effort at explaining away his impatience and curiosity.

"Alright, let's just wait right here out of sight for a bit, before we do any more movin'. That cow'll be waiting for any movement and they'll be gone in a flash. She's what you call the lead cow and makes most of the decisions for the herd."

Sean nodded his head and dropped to one knee to wait. After a few moments, Tate said, "Alright, nock an arrow and we'll move to those willows right there in the bend of the creek. If we can find an opening, I think you can get a shot from there."

Once the boy had his arrow nocked, and Tate did the same, they moved ahead in a crouch, carefully picking their steps. Shortly, they were in place and Tate stood to get a better view of the small herd. Using the thin branches, he was able to see the grazing elk. He was surprised to see there were now about a dozen animals, mostly cows and a few calves and no other bulls. He spotted the spike bull at the near edge of the herd, slowly making his way closer to the creek, snatching mouthfuls of grass as he moved.

"That bull is moving closer to the creek. Get down on your belly and you can see beneath the willows and watch as he comes nearer. When he gets close to the water, then we'll get ready for your shot," instructed his father in a whisper.

Sean bellied down, crawled under the overhanging willows and looked through what appeared to be a rabbit path to see the grazing wapiti. He didn't think the spike bull could move any slower as he grazed on the new sprouts of grass along the creek bank. The loose-jointed jaws of the elk slipped side to side to chew the grass and Sean thought it a little humorous to be watching them eat their dinner while he was hoping to make one of them his dinner. The opposite bank had a wide stretch of willow free grass that marked their usual watering place. There were a couple of cows with their noses in the water and the bull seemed to be waiting his turn. Sean bellied back from the willows and whispered to his father, "I think he'll be getting a drink in a minute. That'll probably be my best shot, don't you think?"

Tate nodded and motioned for him to be ready, "I can see through these thin willows, and when the bull steps to the water and drops his head is when you need to take your shot. You stand right here," he motioned to his left and near the willows, "and when it's time, I'll slowly pull these branches back and you can take your shot."

Sean knew his father also had an arrow nocked, and that he couldn't shoot from where he knelt, but he also knew his dad was very quick with his bow and that gave the boy confidence. The last thing he wanted to happen was to wound an elk and then have to track it down. Sometimes a injured elk could travel many miles before they were downed, and sometimes the wound is not bad enough to do more than bring a little blood. All these thoughts raced through his mind as he stepped to the designated place. With his arm and bow to his side, and his fingers on the string, he nodded to his dad.

Tate motioned for him to ready his shot and Sean lifted the bow, stepped into it as he had been taught and brought the arrow to full draw. Tate knew he couldn't hold the full draw for more than a couple of seconds and as the boy readied himself, Tate slowly moved the branches aside, giving the youngster a clear field of view. The boy brought the arrow into line with the elk, aiming just behind the fore-leg, low on the chest, and as soon as the arrow settled on the mark, he released the feathered missile and it whispered across the creek. Tate stood and brought his bow to full draw as he watched the bull jump when Sean's arrow struck. In that instant, Tate could tell the arrow was a little low, but still penetrated the chest of the bull, but the animal jumped as if on springs, and whirled around to take flight.

The other animals were startled, and heads came up and muscles tensed. Tate let his arrow fly and followed it on its flight to the bull. The elk had started up the slight embankment when the second arrow plunged into its chest, leaving only the fletching protruding, and the bull stumbled to the side, its legs giving out and he fell forward on his neck and chest. The other elk spooked and started to flee toward the thick timber, but a sudden hail of arrows brought down four more elk. The shock of seeing the animals fall was enough, but to see arrows come from nowhere was worse. Then several Indian warriors rose from beyond the willows and brush and started toward their kills. Sean hadn't taken his eyes off the spike bull laying on the bank and looked to his dad with a wide grin, "We got him, Pa, we got him!"

Tate shushed the boy with a hand on his shoulder, then pointed to the Indians. Sean was struck dumb and froze in his tracks, looked to his dad and saw him stand to his full height, and casually nock another arrow, out of sight from the Indians. Tate recognized the hunters as Comanche, but none were known to him and he called out in the Comanche tongue, "Ho, my Comanche brothers, I did not expect to find other hunters here."

While the others went to their kills, one man came toward Tate, bow with a nocked arrow at his side. He lifted one open hand, palm forward, and answered, "We saw you and knew you. Pretty Boy said you were a friend of White Feather and Buffalo Hump. Is that true?"

"Yes, I have been to their village many times, why have I not seen you?" asked Tate.

"Buffalo Hump and White Feather are of the WhahaToya band of the Yaparʉhka Comanche, we are of the Kotsoteka Comanche. We are from the south of Buffalo Hump's band, but the buffalo are few this year, so we must hunt for elk. I am Black Horse."

"And I am Longbow, and this is my son, Bear Chaser."

Black Horse lifted his eyes to the tall white man and said, "These are good names. I have heard of Longbow." He walked forward to clasp forearms in the traditional greeting.

"When I said I was surprised to see you hunting, it is because earlier we saw a hunting party of the Jicarilla coming from here."

"Yes, we saw them too, but they were leaving, so we let them go."

Tate knew that statement could imply many things from hiding out to being too far away for a conflict or perhaps the Comanche knew they were outnumbered and it was best to avoid any contact. But Tate did not address the remark, but instead said, "We will tend to our kill. You are welcome to come to our fire when you are done. I will share my meat with you."

The proper courtesy of the wilderness requires any invitation to be accepted. To do less would be insulting. Black Horse looked at the man, thought for a moment, and nodded his head and said, "We will join you and bring some meat as well."

THE COMANCHE, though friendly enough, were true to what Tate had learned of them. They were known for their warring and raids to take horses and captives. They were excellent horsemen and this band was known to raid to the south into Texas and Mexico, taking horses from farms, ranches, and other tribes. They would then sell the horses to the traders and travelers on the Sante Fe and California trails, and sometimes raid the wagon trains and freighters to steal the horses back. White Feather, the Shaman of the band led by Buffalo Hump, had befriended Tate when he helped their people through the smallpox epidemic the first year that Tate was in the mountains. She had told him about the bands to the south, "They are Comanche, but they are not like us, they cannot be trusted. They will raid and kill to steal horses, then sell or trade them to the whites, only to kill the whites and take them back."

Tate knew he and Sean were safe with the visiting Comanche, it was against their way to disrespect a friend of their people or to insult someone that has shared your fire and your meat. The visit with the hunting party was friendly enough, but a little standoffish and guarded, especially after they saw the wolf in camp. Until one of the warriors, the one known as Broken Wing because of a deformed arm, asked about his name.

"I was given the name by the chief of the Kiowa because of my bow. He was impressed by the size of it and how far it will send an arrow," explained Tate as he lifted his bow from beside him and displayed it for the men to see.

Broken Wing rose and walked closer to see the bow, asking if he could look at it more closely. Tate held the weapon out to him to let him examine it. The warrior stood it beside him and was surprised to see the bow was taller than he was and motioned with his hand at the difference. He spoke to one of his companions, asking for his bow to compare. When he held the two side by side, Tate's bow was at least two feet taller. Broken Wing said, "You cannot use this while riding."

"No, and not just because it is too long, but it is also too hard to draw on horseback," he explained.

"Haw! If a warrior cannot use his weapon from horseback, he is not a warrior!"

Tate looked at the man, then walked toward him and retrieved his bow. He held the string in his hand and using his leg and the opposite toe, he strung the bow. The warriors watched and laughed at the way the white man prepared his bow. Tate reached down to his quiver and brought up an arrow, which caused the men to talk and point because of its length, easily more than a handbreadth longer than theirs, and watched as Tate nocked the arrow. He handed the bow with the arrow to Broken Wing and motioned for him to shoot it. The man shook his head, motioning to his deformed arm, and passed the bow to one of the other Comanche. That man, Howling Wolf, stood and took the bow in hand and began to draw but was surprised at the strength of the weapon. He exerted all his force, obvious to the others by his grimace, and pulled the string to just about a half draw. He released his grip, but just enough to drop the bow without releasing the arrow. He looked at Tate with a shocked expression and handed it back to him. Tate grinned and accepted the bow and sat down.

Black Horse said, "Will you not show us how you shoot this longbow?"

Tate looked to the sky, the full moon casting its spell on the land, and looked to the valley below the camp. He said, "But you will not see how far the arrow goes, it is too dark."

The other warriors also looked around at the light and many spoke at once, all saying it was light enough to see. One even offered to fetch the arrow, so he would not lose it. Tate grinned, having led them on purposefully and after a bit more persuading, finally agreed. Sean knew exactly what his father was doing, and sat beside Lobo, stroking his fur and chuckling to himself.

Tate motioned to the creek in the bottom and said, "That little cluster of aspen, there by the creek."

Black Horse looked where Tate pointed and said, "Haw, that is not far nor hard, even in this light."

Tate smiled and said, "Look beyond the top of the trees, across the creek, there is a dark patch on the hillside there, I think it's flowers. That is what I will shoot."

"Aiieee," said one of the others, "no one can shoot that far. That is two times the range of any bow!" The others laughed but watched Tate as he lifted the bow.

Tate stepped into the bow, pushing with his left arm extended, and brought it to full draw. He lowered the tip of the arrow to just above the target and let the arrow fly. The shaft whispered on its way, surprising the Indians with its flat trajectory, but they quickly lost sight of the arrow in the dim light. They unconsciously leaned forward, squinting their eyes, trying to see where it landed, but failed. Black Horse motioned to the one who volunteered to fetch the arrow, and all watched as he trotted down the slope toward the creek. When he reached the willows, he pushed them aside, searching for the shaft, he looked around and stood facing the others, hands to his side and palms open as he lifted his shoulders to express his failure.

Black Horse looked at Tate as he spoke and motioned, "Tell him to go to the target patch."

The leader of the hunting party shouted his order and the young man turned, waded the creek and trotted up the hill toward the patch. He was but a shadow in the darkness, but they could all see him bend over and turn, holding the arrow over his head and jumping up and down. He started at a run to return and was soon at the fire with the group as they looked at the arrow and back to Tate who stood calmly and unstrung his bow.

The warriors shook their heads in wonder, looked at the bow closely and several held it and fingered it carefully. When they fell silent, it was obvious the Comanche were impressed with this white man and they understood why he was called Longbow. When Sean fell asleep, Lobo at his side, he was smiling with pride, both because of his success and because of his pa.

CHAPTER ELEVEN
CACHES

MICHAEL GARMIN SPENT ANY SPARE TIME RIDING ALONGSIDE the Ritter wagon, talking to Rachel. The two were becoming quite friendly, but Cora did her best to discourage the youthful romance. But Rachel had never lived where there were very many boys, and none her age, except of course her twin brother, and she longed for conversation with the possibility of an even closer friendship. The two laughed often and talked at every opportunity.

Michael had proven himself as a hunter, having spent much time in the woods of Missouri before they left for their journey to the goldfields. Their farm yielded little but rocks and it was necessary for the youth to help out by bringing home the meat, and his mother often said he had a *savoir faire* about hunting. When William Bent saw him bringing in meat on more than one occasion, he enlisted him to do some hunting for the teamsters as well. To gain favor with Rachel, Michael asked Reuben to join him on his hunts and the two had developed an understanding and friendship as they hunted.

Reuben rode up behind Michael and said, "Hey Mike, Mr.

Bent said they could use some more meat for the teamsters. You ready to go?"

The older boy looked back at Reuben, shrugged his shoulders, and replied, "Oh, I guess," and turned to Rachel, "will I see you after supper?"

Rachel smiled and nodded, turned to her mother and asked, "Is that alright, Ma?"

"Long as you're not too far away from the fire, and not gone too long, I reckon it'll be alright." She added a "har-rumph" to express her disapproval but did not change her decree.

Rachel turned back to Michael and said, "Ma said it's alright!" as she smiled broadly at the tousle headed young man. He returned the smile and reined his horse around to join Reuben and the two gigged their horses into a canter to move away from the wagons.

"Mr. Bent said the wagons'll be movin' to the southwest away from the river. He said we could catch up to 'em easy an' the riverbottom'd be the best place to get us a deer."

"I know that. We always hunt the trees an' such along the river. Ain't like we'd find much out here in the flats anyway," he grumbled as he motioned with a wide swinging arm to indicate the empty plains. "Course, there are some antelope and buffalo out there, but ain't none close enough to see, much less shoot!"

Reuben yielded to the older boy in most things, but he had ridden with William Bent for a few weeks. In that time he had learned a lot and definitely felt he was as knowledge-able as Michael about the plains country around them. "If there were buffalo out there, we'd see a big dust cloud first. Can you imagine seein' thousands of 'em at a time? Mr. Bent says some herds are so big it takes days to get around 'em."

"Ah, he's just pullin' your leg, you'll believe anything!"

"Huhuhhhn, I heard some o' the others talkin' 'bout it too.

Maybe we'll see a big herd and get to shoot us a buffalo. They say they're right tasty!" declared Reuben, trying to one-up the older boy.

"What would you know, you're just a kid!" remarked Michael, thinking Reuben needed to be put in his place, after all, he was younger.

Both boys rode in silence until they neared the trees by the river bank. Cottonwood, alder, burr oak, beech, elm and others as well as many shrubs and bushes including willows provided ample shelter for wildlife. The boys were used to seeing turkey, ducks, and a few geese, as well as white tail deer, but their discord made them less than attentive and when they spooked a white tail from the brush, their horses were startled, and the deer trotted off unharmed. They looked at one another and Reuben said, "Guess we need to be payin' attention, ya reckon?"

"Yeah, I reckon," answered Michael. They reined up and looked around, thinking about their hunt and finally Michael said, "Look, I'll get down an' walk the trees, see if I can kick anything out to you. You go down to that point yonder," as he pointed to the trees that stood out from the riverbank, "an' tether the horses and get you a shootin' spot. I'll watch, an' when you're ready, you wave your hat an' I'll go into the trees. I'll be makin' plenty o' noise, so if there's anything in there, they'll either cross the river or head out to the flats. Then you can get a shot. But if I see somethin' I can shoot, I'll do it."

It was a tactic the boys used before and Reuben readily agreed to the plan. Michael stepped down, rifle in hand, and Reuben took the reins to lead his horse away. The point of trees was about a hundred yards away and Reuben was soon slipping from the bay gelding and tethering the horses to a downed cottonwood. He looked around and found another big trunked cottonwood lying just inside the tree line that also gave him a good view of the trees and flats back to the place where Michael stood. Reuben stood, waved his hat and upon seeing Michael start into the trees, he dropped to his knees behind the trunk and lay the muzzle of his rifle across the bare trunk, but not before checking his load and cap. He watched the tree line for any movement and waited.

It was just a few minutes later when Reuben heard the crack of a rifle shot that reverberated through the trees and he knew Michael had taken a shot, probably at a deer. Reuben lifted up just a mite, watching the trees carefully, waiting for any spooked deer to come running from the woods. Suddenly, two does burst from the cover of the trees, running in that bouncing movement that made them look like they were almost floating on air. Reuben brought the sights to bear on the lead doe, followed it for a jump, and when its feet hit the ground again, the rifle bucked and barked, spitting smoke and lead, and the doe fell, flipped end over end, and lay still on its back.

The first rifle shot had emptied the trees of chattering birds, and the second cast a silence upon the scene. As the smoke cleared, Reuben stood, heard the signal whistle from Michael, and started toward the downed deer. The boys had developed a system, if two animals were downed, they would join forces and field dress one at a time, making it easier on both. The whistle told Reuben that Michael had downed his deer and that would be the one to start field-dressing. He quickly reloaded his Hawken and started toward the point he marked in his mind as the place where the shot came from and quietly moved into the woods.

Reuben walked quietly through the trees and brush, careful to pick his way, partly because he had developed the habit of stealthy walking in the woods for hunting, but also because he had a strong aversion to snakes. He cautiously picked each step, always concerned about copperheads and timber rattlers, but he looked up to see Michael already starting to work on the downed deer. But a movement off to the left and behind Michael caught Reuben's eye and he was shocked to see an Indian, trying to sneak up on Michael, with a bow in his hand and an arrow nocked. Reuben stepped beside a slender cottonwood, leaning against it as he brought up his rifle, earing back the hammer all in one motion. He brought the sights to bear just as the Indian was raising his bow and Reuben squeezed off the shot. The rifle bucked and belched smoke as the roar rattled the trees. Michael jumped to the side like he was hit, but seeing Reuben, he looked in the direction of the boy's aim and heard thrashing in the brush. Reuben immediately set to reload his rifle as Michael shouted, "What?"

Reuben answered with a nod of his head, "Indian!" as he pulled the ramrod from the muzzle. He quickly replaced the rod as he started walking toward his friend and searched the brush for the Indian. He placed a cap on the nipple and brought the hammer to full cock, setting the front trigger as he slowly approached. Michael was carefully stepping toward the brush, rifle at the ready before him, and he moved side to side, looking for any movement.

The Indian was dead. Reuben's shot had taken him in the left chest and out the back, killing the warrior before he hit the ground. The boys slowly approached, and Michael poked the Indian's foot, testing to see if he was dead. Suddenly, in the trees beyond they heard the sound of running footsteps, and then the sound of horses thundering away. The boys looked at one another, "There musta been more of 'em," said Michael, stating the obvious.

"What're we gonna do?" asked Reuben, deferring to the older boy.

"Let's get the deer and get outta here, pronto!"

They wasted no time field dressing the animals, getting

the job done faster than they thought possible. After securing the carcasses behind the cantles of the saddles, the two set off at a canter toward the expected rendezvous with the wagons.

When the boys sighted the wagons, they kicked the horses up to a gallop. When they were sighted by Bent, he reined around and trotted his horse to meet the excited boys. As they approached, he called out, "Whoa there, young'uns. Ya' don't need to kill the horses just to get the meat to us, we ain't that hungry." But he saw the big eyes and fast breathing of the boys as well as the animals and he knew there was a problem. When they both started talking at once, Bent held up his hand and said, "Whoa. One at a time, Michael, you first."

"Reuben killed an Indian!" was all he could get out in one breath and started to take another to say more but was stopped by Bent's upraised hand.

Bent looked to Reuben, "You wanna tell me about it?"

"Yeah, I did. But I had to!"

"Yeah, he was gonna shoot me!" interjected Michael.

"Reuben was gonna shoot you?" asked Bent, incredulously.

"No, the Indian!" said the boys in unison.

Bent lifted his head as he looked at the boys, "So, let me get this straight. An Indian was gonna shoot Michael and you," nodding to Reuben, "shot the Indian?"

Both boys nodded their head, relieved to be understood.

"So, how'd you know he was gonna shoot Michael?" Bent asked Reuben.

By this time the boys had settled down somewhat and Reuben took a deep breath and began, "We were in the trees by the river and Michael killed a deer and when the others spooked and ran out, I shot one too. When Michael whistled, that's our signal that we got somethin', I started into the woods to help him dress his deer and that's when I saw the Indian sneakin' up on Michael, so I shot him."

Bent looked to Michael and said, "Sounds like he saved your life."

Michael dropped his head and nodded agreement but said nothing.

Reuben smiled at the thought but then asked, "Am I gonna be in trouble for doin' that?"

"I dunno. I don't think you'll be in any trouble for saving your friend's life, but, tell me, were there any other Indians," asked Bent.

The boys looked at one another and Michael said, "We didn't see them, but we heard at least one running away and then horses running from the trees. Don't know where they went, but we didn't wanna stick around to find out."

Bent chuckled and said, "Well, boys, you did the right thing. But now the Indians know you came from the wagons here and if there's gonna be anything come of you killin' that one, they'll be comin' after the entire train. He turned to look at the passing wagons, stood in his stirrups and shielded his eyes, then looked at the boys. "How 'bout you takin' the meat to Cooky, keep some for your families, and go on back to your wagons. We'll be stoppin' up yonder at the Caches and I'll pass word to the others to stay on their toes cuz we might have visitors."

The boys nodded and gigged their horses toward the wagon driven by the cook of the outfit. After dropping off most of the meat, keeping a hind quarter of each of the animals for their families, the boys trotted back to their wagons to tell the story again to their families and tell them to do as Bent said, and 'stay on their toes' because Bent expected another visit from Indians.

CHAPTER TWELVE
TRADER

Maggie moved the woven willow chair out into the sunshine for the trader to enjoy the day. He was showing improvement every day and Maggie was hopeful the patient would soon be up and about. She sat in her rocker on the porch and busied herself with mending some britches of the boy and thought about her absent men that were off on the first hunt for Sean. She was hopeful they would be successful and bring home some fresh meat, but also for the success of Sean, who had been so excited about his first hunt. And after he got his new bow, he was doubly excited and hopeful of bagging an elk. She remembered the first time she and Tate had gone hunting to give her a try at bagging some game with her bow, and how nervous and excited she was, but after she shot the buck mule deer and walked up to the dead animal with her arrow protruding from his neck, her excitement was replaced with sorrow for the beautiful animal. But she knew the way of the mountains and that survival required them to take the game for their table. After that, she understood the way of the natives, to thank the Creator for the gift of life and to thank the animal for its sacrifice.

The clatter of hooves on the trail leading up to the cabin told of someone's arrival. She stood, lifting her Sharps from its resting place beside the door, and stepped to the top of the porch steps, rifle in hand, watching the trail. When Lobo trotted into the clearing, Maggie sat the rifle back against the wall and pulled her shawl about her shoulders and started down the steps. As the hunters entered the clearing, Sean hollered, "Look Ma!" pointing to the heavy-laden pack-mule, "I got an elk!" He gigged his horse to the corral and slipped from the saddle. He quickly unsaddled the steel dust, put his saddle and blanket in the tack shed, and grabbed a brush to tend to the horse. He looked to see his mother approaching the corral and he turned to her, "Ain't it a beaut, Ma? An' I got him with my bow! Oh, an' you shoulda seen them Indians!" He turned back to brush out his horse, leaving Maggie standing open-mouthed at the fence, awaiting an explanation.

Tate saw her expression and chuckled before he reached through the poles to pull her close. She leaned up on her toes so she could reach above the top rail as Tate bent to kiss his bride. She leaned back and asked, "Indians?"

"Ah, just some Comanche that ate supper with us is all," he answered as he shrugged and turned away to tend to his horse and unload the mule.

Maggie relaxed at his casual attitude and asked, "Were they from White Feather's band?"

"No, they were up from farther south, from the Kotsoteka Comanche, led by Black Horse. He said the buffalo were late in coming north and they needed to hunt elk instead."

Lex Barclay had eased his way from the chair to the corral and stood beside Maggie. He asked, "I've not heard of the Kotsoteka, are they peaceful?"

Tate looked at the trader, surprised to see him standing, "Any Indian that shares your fire is peaceful, and any of 'em can lift your scalp before breakfast, too. But these were peaceable enough, one of the men knew me from the times I've been in White Feather's camp, apparently, he has spent some time there. So, being friends with Buffalo Hump and White Feather helped."

"Ya think I could do some tradin' with 'em?" asked Lex.

Tate finished removing the pack from the mule, the panniers and parfleche were full of meat and the hide had served as a cover over the entire pack. He was thoughtful for a moment and turned to answer the trader, "If I was you, I'd be findin' myself a safer way of livin'. I've been noticin' a general unrest among all the tribes. I never thought any of 'em would attack a white settlement, but after the Christmas massacre at Fort Pueblo, I'm not so sure anymore. Now, I know that bunch wasn't Two Eagles' band, but they were Ute. And the Ute have been the more peaceable tribe of 'em all. I wouldn'ta been surprised if it had been the Apache, but . . ."

"Yeah Ma, we saw some Apache too!" interjected Sean excitedly as he remembered the almost encounter.

Maggie looked to Tate with her hands on her hips and asked, "Apache? Don't tell me you had supper with them too?"

"No, no, we didn't stop to visit with them, we just let 'em go on their way."

Maggie stepped back and waved her arms, "All these mountains and valleys that have deer and elk and you have to take my son into one that has the two meanest bunch of Indians around. I thought you had more sense than that," she declared.

Tate looked at her, laughing, and said, "It does the boy good to get out and meet our neighbors!"

Maggie shook her head and said, "I'm going inside and fix

supper before you tell me there were grizzly bears and mountain lions there too!"

They both knew that anywhere in these mountains there could be any number of perils, not the least of which would be the many different tribes of natives as well as the beasts of the mountains. Tate knew his wife was aware of these things and had even defended her family from many of the dangers, but every so often she had to have the leeway to be a mother. A mother that worried about her children, even though worry never did anyone any good.

"Uh, you were talkin' 'bout the Indians bein' a bit restless?" asked Lex, watching Tate gather up the packs.

Tate stood and looked at the trader, "Yeah, I wouldn't say anything to Maggie, but those Comanche, even though they were bound by the way of their people, they were lookin' over my goods an' it would'na taken much for them to try to slit my throat and take ever'thing. Same with them Apache, even though they were a huntin' party, when they carry their coup sticks with scalps on 'em, they're prepared for any opportunity to add more to their collection."

"Wal, whatta 'boutchu? You got'chur family here an' all, ain'tchu worried 'bout 'em?"

"It's different with us. I've been here for a long time and been friends with most of 'em. And I know they could turn on me at any time, I just don't take unnecessary chances. I've got a good reputation with most all the bands around and have helped some of 'em too. But, if it gets worse, I won't hesitate to get shut o' these mountains an' get my family to safety. They are more important to me than anything and, really, there's nothing that keeps me here. I can build another cabin 'bout anywhere I've a mind too. Matter o' fact, I got me another'n in the Wind River Mountains up north a ways."

"Wal, to be honest with ya', all this sittin' around has had me doin' some thinkin', an' I might take muh mule an' go back to the post at Hardscrabble. I got me a couple more mules an' another horse an' I might just load up the rest o' my stuff, come back here an' pick up what's left of this trip, an' start west. Might not make it all the way to Californy, but I could set up a tradin' post most anywheres. If'n I come acrost some place like ol' Bridger done up north, why, I could do alright."

"You know, if I 'member correctly, after Fremont left, after his little expedition into the San Juans that met with disaster, I believe he went to California by the Old Spanish Trail. Now that don't get too many folks travelin' thataway, but I'm thinkin' you could prob'ly get there with your mules in oh, a month or so. An' they say the weather's plumb nice out there all year 'roun'. A feller could prob'ly get a real nice business set up 'fore all them gold diggers go broke and do purty good for himself."

"By jove, you might have sumpin' there. Humm, I'm gonna hafta do some thinkin' on that. Yessiree."

Maggie called her men to supper and while Tate and Sean packed the gear into the house, Lex followed along behind using a walking stick he fashioned during his idle hours in the sunshine. Following the meal of fresh elk steak, potatoes, and squaw cabbage, Maggie surprised the men with a big mountain berry pie made with an assortment of strawberries, raspberries and chokecherries she had gathered the last couple of days. Everyone raved about the rare treat and when the men pushed away from the table, Maggie drafted the two youngsters as helpers on cleanup duty.

Tate and Lex stepped out onto the porch and took seats to enjoy the sunset over the San Juans. Tate began, "You remember Fremont, don't you?" he asked of Lex.

The man chuckled and said, "Doesn't ever'body in these hyar mountains? I mean, after all, what that man tried that cost so many lives, yeah, we ain't about to forget that dumb pilgrim!"

Tate dropped his head as he remembered the time he spent with the man known as the Pathfinder, preferring to forget the time. "What I was gonna say, you know he came back through here last year, and he went o'er the Cochetopa Pass an' down through the Gunnison valley. He made it all the way to California, takin' what's been called the northern route of the Old Spanish Trail. They say he spent time out there in Mormon country in a settlement called Parowan. I s'pose, if'n you'd prefer that route, you could prob'ly set up shop in that town an' wouldn't hafta go all the way to California."

"Hah! I've heerd some stories 'bout them Mormons. I know they's just like other folks an' there's good 'uns and bad 'uns, but even ol' Bridger's been havin' problems with 'em. Nosir, I'd just as soon not stick muh nose where it don't belong. If'n I go anywheres, it'll prob'ly be that southern route you spoke of. So, here's what I'm thinkin', soon's I can handle muh mule, I'm gonna do like I said an' go fetch the rest o' muh stuff. An' I'll come back hyar an' fetch whut you gathered up fer me, an' if'n by that time, I still got the itchy feet, then I'll skedaddle o'er them trails and go see that thar ocean." He nodded his head to emphasize his decision and grinned up at Tate.

Tate looked at the man that had been his friend for many years and slowly let a grin paint his face, "I do believe you'll do it. And I think it'll be a good thing for you, too."

CHAPTER THIRTEEN
BUFFALO

IT WAS A QUIET NIGHT FOR THE WAGON TRAIN, THE EXPECTED attack from whatever band of Indians that lost their hunter never came, much to the relief of everyone. Bent was an experienced traveler of the Sante Fe Trail and knew that none of the Indians that claimed the territory as their own could be counted on to do what was expected. He had the train on the move at first light and made certain every wagon had rifles ready..

The custom on wagon trains was to rotate the lead. Whichever wagon was in the lead the day before would drop back and the one from the end of the train would move to the front, giving everyone a time in the lead and out of the dust of the rest of the wagons. Today was the day the Ritter wagon yielded their place in the lead and fell back to second in line. Reuben was riding with William Bent well ahead of the train but behind the scout who rode a mile or two, and often more, ahead of the winding, slow-moving train. Scouting was not a job for the inexperienced and Bent used an experienced former mountain man and trapper called

Uncle Dick Wooton, who had scouted for several of his trips to and from the east.

The wagons were making good time and were about seven miles west of the Caches when Uncle Dick came riding back at a gallop and slid to a stop beside Bent. "Might have a problem yonder," he said as he twisted around in his saddle and motioned with his rifle to the west. "There's a purty good dust cloud," he twisted around again, "ya can see it thar, just south o' the river. Looks like it's a big herd o' buff! But that ain't the problem, cuz I spotted some Injuns, Comanche I think, hidin' themselves in the trees on this side o' the river. Now, best I can figger it is they got other'ns tryin' to push the buffler 'crost the river and these'll shoot 'em comin' up outta the water. That's the best figgerin', the worst is these'ns are different from whoever's kickin' up the herd and they're gonna ambush 'em. Or, they could just be layin' in the brush an' waitin' fer the wagons. Any way ya look at it, don't look good fer us."

Bent stood in his stirrups, shaded his eyes, straining to see any sign of the Indians or the herd. He looked around the flats, the river and the greenery that marked the river course was to their left and the plains rolled away to the horizon to the west and north. A slight knoll was off to their right and Bent handed the reins of his horse to Reuben and motioned for Uncle Dick to follow as he trotted to the knoll, brass telescope in hand.

Once atop the knoll, Bent sat down, drew up his knees and used them to stabilize his telescope as he looked to the tree-line beyond. Although he couldn't see any of the warriors hidden in the brush, he could make out their horses being held by a couple of young men back away from the obvious river crossing. He lifted the scope to the boiling dust cloud and was unable to make out any riders behind the herd, but he knew if there was anyone in that maelstrom of prairie dust, they might not be seen for several hours after the cloud settled. Bent looked to the scout, "I'm purty sure they ain't waitin' on us, their horses are not hidden, but just bein' held outta the way. They're either waitin' for the herd, or for whoever's got 'em moving. My money's on the herd. If they hit 'em comin' outta the water, they'd have some easy shootin'."

Bent stood and started back to his horse and said, "You know, we could use some fresh buffalo meat. Mebbe I'll have a couple shooters take up a spot an' take us a couple of them wooly boogers."

"Don'tchu think that'll make them Injuns a little mad? Shootin' their buffler?"

"Nah, not if we get a couple extry for 'em. Might go a long way to makin' friends an' keep 'em off our tail the rest o' the way."

Uncle Dick just looked at Bent, wondering if the man had a few screws loose in his head thinking you could buy off any Indian with a couple of buffalo. But he chose to keep his thoughts to himself, after all, Bent had traveled this country just as much as he had and had proven himself a good nego-tiator with the different tribes. Uncle Dick was just hoping this was one of the tribes that Bent had good relations with, because if he didn't, well . . .

When Bent and Reuben approached the wagons, Bent signaled for them to circle up and make camp for the night. Although mid-morning and they had only traveled no more than five or six miles since their camp of the night before, most were thinking they were under attack. Everyone quickly went through the motions of preparing for an attack, until Bent sent Reuben to explain to the each wagon that the stop was due to a buffalo herd crossing the river about a half mile beyond their stop.

While Reuben made the rounds, William Bent went directly to the Ritter wagon to talk with Cora and Rachel. He tipped his hat and began, "Ladies, if you're of a mind, we could use your sharpshooter skills up yonder at the river crossing. There's a herd of buffalo headin' thataway," he turned and motioned to the distant dust cloud, "and when they cross the river, that'd be a good time to get us some fresh meat. Have you ever had any buffalo?"

Cora looked suspiciously at the leader of the train and cocked one eyebrow, "Cain't say as we have."

"Well, it's mighty tasty and they're big enough to feed us for a while. If you ladies would put those big Sharps to use and bring down a couple of 'em, we'd all be grateful. Course we could bag one or two with the Hawkens or other rifles, but it's mighty easy to wound one o' them critters and make 'em mad atchu. But with those big Sharps and your fine shootin', well, I don't think you'd have any trouble. If you drop 'em, I'll have my men do the dressin' out of 'em."

Cora looked to Rachel and the girl just shrugged her shoulders, letting her mother make the decision. She looked back to Bent, "I reckon we can do that. Do I just drive muh wagon up there?"

"No, I'll get one o' my wagons an' a couple fellers to go and you can ride with them. You just leave your wagon here, an' I'll have some o' my men unhitch your team an' such, an' Reuben an' I will go along as well. You just wait an' I'll be right back." He reined his horse around and started toward the first of his wagons. When he returned, both Reuben and Michael Garmin followed, as did the wagon with two freighters and a helper. The women climbed aboard, with rifles in scabbards, possibles bags hanging over their shoulders, and each carrying a bipod for a shooting rest.

Reuben and Michael rode up alongside the wagon and asked, "Ma, did Mr. Bent tell you 'bout the Indians?"

The woman snapped her head in Reuben's direction, fire flaming in her eyes, "Indians? No, he didn't! You go get that man an' tell him I wanna talk to him, now!" As Reuben reined his horse around, Cora mumbled to herself and it sounded something like she was going to shoot Bent instead of any buffalo. Rachel just looked at her mother, well aware of the woman's fiery temperament, and looked back toward Michael who chose not to follow Reuben but to stay near his girl.

Rachel smiled at the young man and asked, "Are you going to shoot some buffalo too?"

"Nah, Mr. Bent just wanted some more rifles along just in case, you know."

"Just in case the Indians weren't too happy with us?" she asked.

"Somethin' like that, I guess. But, I'm sure he knows what he's doin', he usually does."

Rachel lifted her head and looked around without responding to the boy's observation. The tree-line by the river, if it could be called that, was sparse with many different trees and bushes, but no area was thick with vegetation as to prevent the banks to not be easily seen. The rising dust cloud was nearing the river and Bent motioned to the freighter with the lines to hurry up and take the place chosen for the wagon. When the freighter pulled the wagon perpendicular to the thicker trees, Rachel saw the small horse herd and the young warriors beside them. It was obvious the tenders were nervous about the coming white men and Reuben saw one had already trotted off toward the wider break in the trees that marked the river crossing.

Bent tethered his horse to the wagon and came to assist the women down, taking their rifles and other gear before offering his hand to assist. As soon as Cora's feet hit the ground she turned on Bent, "What about them Injuns?!" She stood with hands on her hips and feet spread as if she was ready to take a swing at the man.

But he stopped her when he said, "You won't be shootin' 'til after they take their shots. They're up there in the brush and will be hittin' the buff just as soon's they come outta the water. After the rest o' the herd passes 'em by, that's when you two will do your shootin'. An' all we need is a couple o' them nice fat cows or young bulls, but you might take a couple extry that we can give to them as a peace offerin'. You know where to shoot 'em?" he asked.

"Yup," and turning to Rachel she explained, "It's just like any other big 'un. Best shot's in the heart, right behind the front legs an' low in the chest." She turned to Rachel and nodded, looked at the flats and the crossing and motioned to a small clump of sage and said, "We'll set up there." She took the rifle from Bent and started to the brush, followed by Rachel.

They dropped to one knee and set the bipods before them, lay the muzzle of their rifles in the two-legged support and readied themselves to shoot, just as the herd hit the water at the crossing. There was bellowing from the beasts that burst from their lowered muzzles as they crashed into the water. The leaders wanted to stop and take a drink but were pushed on by the tide of brown behind them. The splashing of water, the grunting of the beasts, the clatter of hooves on stone, the rattle of horns crashing together, all made for a cacophony of noise unlike any the women had ever heard. The excitement rose, and the first arrows flew, and shots sounded from the hidden hunters in the brush. The cloud of smoke from the rifles mixed with the dust and the blast of the muskets added to the exhilaration and the ground shook as the massive herd pushed across the river and climbed the low rising bank as the beasts searched for an escape.

They saw several animals fall, some to be trodden under the hooves of hundreds, and the brown shaggy mass with black eyes flashing, tongues slobbering, noses blowing muddy snot, and bellowing their protests came onward. The women started and with the men standing beside them, began to follow the targets that came into their sights.

The first boom of the big .52-50 Sharps came from Cora's rifle, stabbing the air with a lance of grey smoke that launched the big slug. A puff of dust on the shaggy brown hide of her first target marked the hit. The young bull stumbled, banging against another beside him, staggered several more steps before sliding on his chin, plowing a furrow into the dirt. Another blast sounded and Rachel's rifle spit flame and a big cow had her front feet buckle under her and she flipped end over end and slid to a stop, making two others behind her swerve to miss the big obstacle in their path. Both women quickly dropped their levers to open the breeches, pulled out the refuse and inserted another paper cartridge, lifted the levers and put caps on the nipples as they lifted the rifles for another shot.

The women's rifles blasted again, and more beasts fell, and it was like a tide pushed against the herd, making them move away from the death dealing buffalo guns. After quickly reloading, Cora looked to Bent and he motioned them back to the wagon. The men ushered the women, carrying their bipods, as they trotted back to the wagon, well back from the thundering mass of the wooly beasts. It was easily an hour before the herd had dwindled and the stragglers passed them by, and the butchering crew could set about their task. When the men started to the downed animals, Bent suggested the women wait in the shade of the wagon while the men did the "dirty work." Cora nodded and seated herself beside the big back wheel and stretched out her legs as she motioned for Rachel to join her.

William Bent walked slowly toward the Indians that were now approaching their kills. He had one hand lifted and was unarmed, save for his sidearm that was out of sight under his buckskin jacket. He was watched by all of the Indians as he approached, he had recognized the hunters to be Comanche and he called out a greeting in their native tongue. He identified himself and several of the hunters nodded their heads in recognition, as many of the Comanche had traded at Bent's Fort. As he neared, two of the warriors had already split open one of their kills and brought out a big cut of liver. The others looked to the visitor and motioned for him to join them. Bent obliged and was offered a slice of the liver, as several others had already taken. It was the custom to take the liver from a fresh kill, dip slices into the bile and eat it as a delicacy and celebration of the kill. Those that had already eaten had bloody hands and chins and were grinning at the white man to see if he would partake. Bent grinned, nodded his head, and accepted the liver, put it to his mouth to take a big bite, used his knife to slice it off at his lips, and handed the liver the warrior beside him. The others shouted and nodded their approval and the group began to talk and brag of their kills.

It was usually the custom among the tribe that women would accompany them on a buffalo hunt, but because these were of the Kotsoteka band and they were far from their village, the men had to do the butchering and the cooking that would follow. It was also their custom to invite all the hunters to the feast, but without the women to do the work, the invitation was not extended. As this was explained to the white man, he chuckled, "Uh, yeah, but as you see, it is the men of our group that are doing the butchering. But did you see it was two women that killed the buffalo? And they killed three more as our gift to you for allowing us to join your hunt."

The leader of the band stepped back and examined the white man's expression to see if he was truthful, and asked, "Women? Women did the shooting?"

Bent nodded, his head smiling.

"Why? Do you not shoot?" asked the leader, who had introduced himself as Black Buffalo.

Bent chuckled and said, "Yes, but these women have shoots far rifles and they are very good. The big guns they use are very deadly."

"I would see these women, and these rifles they shoot," he asked and Bent nodded and motioned for the man to follow.

When they stepped around the wagon, Cora and Rachel were surprised to see Bent accompanied by an Indian. The man stood before them, arms crossed over his bone breast-plate and looked at the women. Cora and Rachel stood and looked back at the man, and Cora cocked one eyebrow and tilted her head as she looked the man over as if he was a horse she would be buying. Black Buffalo had broad shoulders, a braided strap with beaded fringe around his upper arm, long black hair with two notched feathers at the back, and a beaded breechcloth that matched the beaded design on his moccasins. He was an impressive figure who turned to Bent and asked, "Where are these rifles you spoke of that shoot so far?"

Bent spoke to Cora, "He would like to see your rifle." She nodded and handed the rifle to the Indian, watching carefully as he examined it. Black Buffalo asked in his tongue, and Bent translated, "Can he shoot it?"

Cora nodded, stepped closer and showed the man how to cock the hammer and set the triggers. The man did as shown and lifted the rifle to his shoulder to take aim. He motioned to a big rock about two hundred yards distant, aimed and pulled the trigger. The big rifle bucked and rocked the man back on his heels. His big eyes showed his astonishment and he looked to see where his shot had gone. But his amazement kept him from seeing clearly and Bent said, "Good shot!" although the bullet had gone well wide of the target. The Indian smiled and handed the rifle back to Cora.

He turned away from Cora and spoke excitedly to Bent. William looked to Cora and tried to keep from smiling but failed as he answered the warrior. The very animated conversation continued with many gestures from the Indian and several looks back to the women. Bent laughed and shook his head and finally convinced the Indian the conversation was finished. The man looked again at Cora, Rachel, and the rifles and walked away shaking his head.

"Now, what was that all about?" asked Cora as Bent turned back to them.

He laughed again, looked to Cora and said, "He wanted to trade for you two and your rifles."

"What?!" she blustered.

"Yup, he got up to twenty horses for the two of you and your rifles, but I told him if I sold you, you'd probably shoot me before you left the wagons."

"You've got that right! But he was sayin' somethin' like he was callin' me some kinda name, he kept sayin' it over an' over, what was that?"

Bent chuckled again and said, "He called you a Wapiti Widow."

"What's a Wapiti Widow?"

"Well, in the fall the elk or Wapiti bulls gather up their harem and take care of 'em and come spring, they leave 'em. The cows have their calves and don't get together again with the bulls till next fall. So, when a woman has a man and he leaves her with children, the Indians call that a Wapiti Widow."

"Hummpph," growled Cora as she climbed up into the wagon to wait for the men to load the meat and return to the train.

When Rachel joined her, the girl giggled a little and said, "Humm, a Wapiti Widow huh, that's interesting."

"Ain't neither nohow, an' I don't wanna hear no more 'bout it," declared the woman.

CHAPTER FOURTEEN
ARRIVAL

It was late on the seventh day after the buffalo hunt, the blinding sun rested on the western horizon and shared its brightness with the underbelly of scattered clouds that dotted the fading blue like tufts of dirty cotton. The train wound its way along the north bank of the Arkansas and slowly climbed the rise that held the silhouetted image of Bent's Fort at Big Timbers. As the wagons crested the hill, the fort sat on the promontory of the river bank and stood tall overlooking the entire plains. Its sixteen-foot high walls of sandstone, parapets with cannon, and a massive gate on the northwest facing wall showed its strength. Several Indian lodges were scattered on the flats to the north and west, with cookfires burning and children running around, mostly naked, and women busy at their tasks of cooking and working with hides.

It was the first semblance of civilization seen by those of the wagons since the three-structure village of Council Grove, almost three weeks back. Cora's wagon was near the middle of the line, driven by Reuben, as Rachel and their mother stood behind him looking at all the lodges and natives. They saw William Bent rein up his horse next to a lodge where a woman and two youngsters stood waiting. Bent quickly slipped from his horse and embraced the woman and hugged the two children. As they stood talking, a young man and young woman, dressed as the other natives, approached and the young woman hugged Bent and the young man clasped forearms with him. Cora said, "That must be his family. He said he had two boys and two girls still with their mother, plus the boy he took back east to school. I thought they were all young'uns, but 'pears two of 'ems a mite older."

Reuben said, "The young boy's name is Charley, I forget what it is in Cheyenne, but it means White Hat. He's younger'n me, but the girl's the same age."

Cora looked at her son, "You'n him musta done a lotta talkin' when you was ridin' fer you to know all that 'bout him and his'ns."

"Nah, not so much. He said I reminded him of his son, Charley."

Bent had directed the wagons to circle up in the clearing to the north of the fort beside the lodges of the Arapaho. There were four wagons already settled there, and the six wagons of the California bound gold seekers joined the small group. George Garmin had assumed the leadership of the six from Missouri and when everyone was situated, teams unhitched, and cookfires going, he went from wagon to wagon to let everyone know that Bent would meet with them after they had their supper.

As the pilgrims assembled, Garmin introduced the other families, "These are the Greene's," and as he introduced each family, he walked around to point them out, "and the O'Toole's, and the Whitman's and the Eichmann's." He then walked to the group that had clustered in front of their wagons and were seated on an assortment of stools, benches, and boxes. "And these are the Ritter's, the Honeycutt's, the Northrup's, the Cutler's and the Simpson's and of course this is my wife and son, Edna and Michael."

When the introductions were finished, Bent stepped into the firelight and began, "Well folks, this is where we part company. As you know, I'll be staying here with my family and this is my home," he motioned around to the fort and village of the Cheyenne, "and you folks are wanting to go farther west. Now, in a couple of days, there'll be six of my wagons that'll be headin' north to take some goods to Fort St. Vrain and anybody that wants to go that way, you'll be welcome to tag along. That will get you closer to the Oregon Trail an' if you wanna join up with another wagon train, then you can. There will also be some wagons headin' south to Sante Fe. Now from down yonder you can catch the Old Spanish Trail, southern route, an' that'll take you to California. An' if'n any o' you want, you can head out from here on your own an' go o'er them mountains yonder and catch the northern route of the Old Spanish Trail an' that'll take you to California also."

Garmin stepped forward and asked, "Which route is the shortest to the goldfields?"

"That'd be the north route of the Old Spanish Trail, that'll take you direct west fer a spell an' after you get o'er the Sangre de Cristos, it'll turn north and o'er some more mountains, although they're a mite smaller, and then due west."

"Are there any Indians?" asked Harold Greene, the captain of the smaller group.

Bent chuckled and said, "There's Indians ever'where. But if you're askin' are there any Indians on the trails, well, on the southern route there's Comanche and Apache. The northern route there's Comanche, Apache, and Ute. An' if'n you're thinkin' goin' north with my wagons, there's Ute, Arapaho, and Cheyenne. And of course, them's just the first Indians you might run into, go much further an' there's others."

"Are we gonna need a guide?" asked Frank Simpson, the bookkeeper from Missouri.

"It's always best, but several folks have made it without a guide. Some head out and pick up a guide along the way, but I could give you the basic directions if need be."

The evening continued with questions, answers, speculations and discussions. Bent left and the conversation continued, but Cora and her two quietly walked away to return to their wagon.

"So, Ma, what're we gonna do?" asked Reuben, voicing the question both were thinking.

"Well, the way I see it, all o' them's mighty anxious to get to the goldfields an' they'll be wantin' to take the fastest way which, according to what Bent said, is the one that goes due west into them mountains he called the Sangre de Cristos. An' that don't leave us with much choice, cuz it sure sounds like they's a lotta Injuns no matter which way we go, howsomever, we don't hafta go to Californy, we could go just 'bout anywhere we wanted. We could go south to Sante Fe and set up shop an' make a home there, but from what Bent says, we'd hafta learn how to speak that there Spanish. An' there ain't much'a nuthin' north o' here, but there's some places 'tween here'n Californy. An' we could go on to see the ocean. What'chu two think?"

Reuben and Rachel looked at one another, surprised their mother would even ask them, she never had before. But Rachel spoke up, "I think we should go on to California. I'd like to see the ocean!"

Reuben quickly replied, "You just wanna go wherever Michael does!"

"That's not true, but so what if it is?"

Reuben didn't answer his sister but looked to his ma, "It'd prob'ly be safer to travel with the rest o' the wagons, don'tchu think?"

"Ummhumm, prob'ly," answered his mother, non-committedly.

They turned in for the night, knowing commitments wouldn't be needed until in the morning and theirs would depend on the decision of the rest of the train. Morning would come soon enough, and they would also need to resupply before going any further, no matter what direction.

The Ritter's were sitting around their fire, finishing their morning meal, when they were approached by George Garmin and Harold Greene.

"Mrs. Ritter, this is Harold Greene, he's the captain of the group of wagons we will be joining up with."

Cora looked at the man from under her scowled brow and answered, "Mr. Greene."

"Mrs. Ritter, I understand you're traveling without a man, is that correct?"

"Not that it's any o' yore bizness, but that's correct."

"Isn't that a little odd? Don't you think you should have a man?"

"Why? You volunteerin' fer the job?"

The man sputtered and stammered, "Uh no, of course not! But most women wouldn't want to risk going through Indian country and traveling all this way by themselves. I'm not sure it would be a good idea to have a woman alone travelin' with our wagons."

Cora set aside her tin plate and coffee cup, stood with hands on her hips as she looked at the man who stood head and shoulders above her. "Wal, first off, I don't recall askin' yore permission to do anything, an' I ain't certain I'd wanna travel with a bag o' wind that thinks he knows more'n everybody else anyway! As fer travelin' by myself, I ain't, cuz I got muh boy and Rachel here an' I'm willin' to bet either one of 'em can outshoot you any day o' the week. So's far as I'm concerned, I ain't the one that needs protectin'!"

"Well, well, I just . . ." stammered the captain.

Garmin quickly stepped in and said, "Uh, maybe you should know that when we fought off the Kiowa, Cora and her young'uns did more to defend the wagons than any of us. Matter o' fact, she an' her daughter there made quite a long shot and dropped the chief, which sent the rest of the band on their way."

The captain looked from Garmin to the Ritter family and back again, "Well, why didn't you say that in the first place? Let me make a fool of myself like you done, humph.!"

He turned away and started to leave but heard Cora say, "Don't think you needed much help to do that!"

THEY WERE on their way west by midday, with everyone re-supplied, wagons and harnesses checked, and water barrels filled. The younger men were assembled under the direction of Marilyn Cutler's brother, Alfred Mays, as the scouting party. And he wisely partnered them up with each member having the opportunity to get acquainted with those from the other wagons. Harold Greene and George Garmin would share the duties of captain or wagon master. Everyone was excited to begin this leg of their trip to the goldfields and spirits were high and everyone was friendly. It promised to be a good trip, even though they preferred to have a guide. They tried to convince Uncle Dick Wooton to take on the job, but he wasn't interested in going where 'all them crazy miners would be diggin' in the dirt.'

"Ma, do you think it'll be alright, not having a guide, I mean?" asked Rachel as she sat beside her mother on the wagon seat. Cora was busy with the lines and occasionally picked up her buggy whip to get the mules' attention, but she turned to her daughter and said, "Girl, one thing you need to learn. That is, you should always be ready to do whatever needs to be done, whether there's a man around or not. Just cuz you're a woman, don't mean you can't tend to things yourself. Now, the only reason we're travelin' with this bunch is cuz there's safety in numbers. Ain't cuz there's a bunch o' men that think they can do anythin' better, cuz they cain't. We'll prob'ly hafta bail 'em outta trouble more'n once 'fore this trip's over. But, that bein' said, Mr. Bent tol' me 'bout a man that might be of help, name o' Tate Saint. He lives up there in them mountains an' he's been known to help folks now'n then. So, we might get us guide anyway."

"That'd be good, wouldn't it ma?"

"We'll see, mebbe so. We'll just wait'n see what happens. Ya never know what's just 'round the bend, now do'ya?"

"No, I suppose not."

Rachel fell into a melancholy mood thinking about their future, especially hers, and wondered if that might include Michael. She smiled at the thought but was brought out of her reverie when she heard her brother's voice, "Hey you two! What's for supper?"

Rachel looked at her brother, "Whatever you bring us! And I don't see any fresh meat behind that saddle, so you better get to huntin' us up some!"

He waved his hat to his sister and gigged his horse around and started off into the flats at a canter. He had seen some antelope and thought he might be able to bag one of the elusive creatures and have something different for supper. He was feeling more like a man than the thirteen-year-old youngster he really was, although he had shown a spurt of growth on the trip and now stood less than a hand width shy of six feet. He was growing out of all his clothes and he hoped he could get either Ma or his sister to put their sewing skills to work on his behalf. But first, they needed some meat.

CHAPTER FIFTEEN
COMANCHE

THE SERENE APPEARANCE OF THE VILLAGE WAS TYPICAL FOR A mid-summer afternoon, with several women gathered around the few fresh elk-hides, scraping and talking as they worked. Children were scrambling to and fro, some chasing willow hoops with sticks, attempting to keep them rolling, giggling and shouting all the while. Several men were working in the shade of the taller pines, fashioning arrows from the cured alder shafts, others knapping flint and splitting feathers for fletching. The grey-haired elders sat in the shade of the lodges, watching the others and offering advice to any who would listen. Older women tended to pots of stew that filled the air with delightful aromas. The meadowlarks chirped their songs into the peaceful quiet of the trees, only to be argued about among the squirrels that twitched their way from limb to limb.

The sudden flutter of wings as a flock of whiskey jacks took flight gave warning of visitors. Several of the men reached for their weapons, always close at hand, some for rifles others for lances and war clubs and still others for bows and newly crafted arrows. Their moves to stand or take cover showed no fear or alarm, just preparedness. A shout from the scouts on the perimeter of the camp told of no cause for alarm and everyone returned to their tasks.

Two of their own rode into the camp at a canter and slid from their mounts near the lodge of their leader, Raven. He was the brother of White Feather, the shaman of the people, and their father, Buffalo Hump had crossed over several years prior. Raven had become the respected leader of this WhahaToya band of the Yaparʉka Comanche and he had ruled them well. The riders were Fat Porcupine and Running Buffalo, scouts that had been sent to search for the anticipated move of the buffalo. Their excitement made the young warriors talk over each other as they gave the news.

"The buffalo are moving! They are coming up the valley beyond the mountains!" declared Porcupine.

"It is a large herd, and they are moving slow. They are this side of the big river," added Buffalo.

Raven stood before them, black braids hanging over his broad shoulders, arms crossed before his chest, and asked, "You say they are moving slow, will the village have time to overtake them for a hunt?"

"Yes, when we spotted them, they were south of Purgatoire creek and moving slow, no dust cloud followed," answered Porcupine, as Buffalo nodded in agreement.

"Good, tell everyone we will move today and go to the pass of Sangre Ccreek to go into the valley and hunt. We must move now," pronounced the chief, before turning back to his lodge to tell his woman to ready his weapons. Running Buffalo trotted to the lodge of White Feather, as his duty as her apprentice was to help her in all things and there would be much to do with her many herbs, plants, medicines and other paraphernalia.

Within moments of the announcement, buffalo hide lodges were slipping from the tipi poles, travois were readied, and packs were assembled as the young men brought the horses into the camp. Even the dogs had packs as everyone stepped to their assigned tasks and the village was on the move by early afternoon. An air of excitement was seen in all the activity and shouted instructions, the attitude was one of eagerness and anticipation of the coming hunt. The summer buffalo expedition was the most important hunt of the year as most of the meat and others needs would be the product of a successful hunt. The meat would be smoked and cured, some made into pemmican, but all laid up for use during the long winters in the mountains.

As the caravan took shape and began to move, scouts were sent before and behind and to each of the flanks, and the snake of the village could only be viewed in its entirety from some lofty mountain-side escarpment. It was only the broad winged golden eagle floating on the cool updraft of air that could see the brown horde of the buffalo herd shuffling its way north on the west side of the mountains, and the eager members of the village with almost a hundred lodges that raised a narrow strip of dust along the headwaters of the Cuchara River that paralleled the east side.

———

THE FIVE SCOUTS and their leader, Alfred Mays, were with George Garmin and Harold Greene, the two co-captains, each holding a steaming cup of coffee as they sat around the fire near the Greene's wagon. Gertrude Greene had just lifted the lid off the dutch oven and was passing the biscuits around the circle of men.

George Garmin was on one knee and had a stick in hand as he drew in the smoothed-out dirt. "Now, the way Bent told it, we're to follow the Cuchara River," and he motioned to a squiggly line in the dirt, "here. Then we'll be followin' the feeder creek of the river, here. The trail just north of the river, which we been followin', will take us 'tween them Spanish Peaks yonder," and he motioned with his stick to the south at the two peaks they had been looking at for the last six days, "and the Wet Mountains along here." He pointed to the shoulder of foothills behind him. "He said the Sangre de Cristos are west o' them Wet Mountains and the pass he called LaVeta Pass will take us through here." He nodded to their west and up the wide valley that lay before them. "When we near the top, he said the road switches back on itself a couple times an' goes o'er the top and from up there we'll see the San Luis Valley beyond. Now, if we make good time, we should get o'er it today, but if it gets a little difficult, we might end up campin' up on top and not get into the valley till tomorrow. Everyone understand?" He looked around to all the scouts, the young men of the train, and added, "Well, when you're scoutin', as always, keep your eyes peeled for Injuns. I'm hopin' we can sneak through here and be into the valley 'fore we run into any. So, if'n there's no questions, let's get ta' movin'." He stood to dismiss the others and Alfred Mays picked Matthew Honeycutt and Hank Greene to be the scouts to start the day. The others went to their wagons and families to help get under way.

Reuben gladly took the reins of their wagon, relieving his mother from the task she had handled most of the trip. The horse was tied to the back of the wagon and would have a leisurely stroll to keep up, rather than the usual work out as a scout.

"Accordin' to what Mr. Garmin's sayin', we might make it o'er the pass today and get an even better look at them mountains. Ain't they sumpin' Ma?"

"They are, never thought they could be so big. I'd heard some folks talk about 'em, but those few what seen 'em, just didn't have words 'nuff to tell 'bout 'em." She sat beside her son on the wagon seat and with one foot on the side board she looked to the mountains that rose on both sides of the trail. "One o' them freighters said he'd seen it snow on them mountains in the middle of summer!"

"I can't imagine it snowin' in the middle o' summer. But, I know the air last night was a mite cooler than it has been since we left Missouri," said Rachel, from behind her mother. She had fashioned a seat with a board across the wagon sides and tied down with twine.

"I just hope we don't run into any Indians! Mr. Bent said there were Comanche, Apache and Ute thisaway. I know them Comanche we shared the buffalo with were peaceable enough, but, I don't know . . ." said Reuben shaking his head.

Cora reached for her Sharps that stood in the corner by her feet, lifted it to check the load and cap. Her movement made Rachel do the same and ask, "You want me to check your rifle too, Reuben?"

"Oh, I'm sure it's alright, but check it anyway. Can't be too careful, I reckon."

Cora smiled at her youngsters that were growing up mighty fast on the journey west. She was pleased they were together and she was proud of the way the twins had risen to their responsibilities. She was a little concerned about the friendship between Rachel and Michael, but she knew she had to let the girl learn to make her own choices, even though some of those choices would be wrong and hurtful. She thought about the other families on the train. When they came from Missouri with the freighters, those in the wagons kept to themselves and hadn't really come to know one another. But since they left the fort, she was learning a lot about those that made up this much smaller train.

She had observed the changes in each of the families. Like the Garmin's; George had shown himself to be a strong man, concerned about others and protective of his own, but early on he seemed to be a quiet man that kept to himself and didn't involve himself in the needs of anyone but his family. And the Simpson's; Mildred had shown herself to be the boss of that family and her husband Frank the milquetoast type that only did what he was told, but now he seemed to be coming out of his shell and would occasionally speak up about things. And each of the other families, some showing themselves to be less or more than thought and some changing dramatically. Sidney Northrup seemed the decent sort, but he was showing his darker side by trying to bully some of the others. Mr. Bent was right when he said the west changes people, the wide-open spaces and the lack of any kind of law or restraints brought out the best and worst in people.

The crack of the buggy whip in the hands of Reuben brought Cora from her musing and she looked around to see the valley was closing in on them, the hills rising more steeply on both sides. To their left, down in the bottom, was the unnamed feeder creek of the Cuchara River, mostly hidden by the willows and other brush, but just past the stream, forested hillsides thick with spruce and fir rose steeply with ravines and rocky outcroppings scarring the slopes. To their right the hillside was also marked with rocks, gullies, and scattered juniper and piñon and thick oak brush rose to a long bald white ridge that stretched beyond their sight. To the farmers from Missouri, it was an amazing view, beyond any they had imagined.

George Garmin signaled the wagons to bunch up and pull alongside one another in a wide area where a draw from the white topped mountain held a wide arroyo that gave them room. The climb up the rugged incline was beginning to show the pilgrims just how difficult it might be to get over these mountains, and Garmin told everyone to take their animals to water in the nearby creek and give them a chance to get a little graze on the grassy banks.

"The rest of the pull up this pass is goin' to be purty hard on 'em, so let 'em get some rest and some grass. We'll take a couple hours for our nooner."

Even though everyone was anxious to get over the pass, the break was a welcome one and the families broke out the left-overs from breakfast and several stretched out on the grassy slope above the trail. The cedars and piñons offered little enough shade, but what was there was a welcome respite for everyone. Most knew that if the climb up the pass was as difficult as Garmin implied, they would be walking the rest of the way.

Michael Garmin walked back to the Ritter wagon and saw Rachel and Reuben sitting below an oak brush. Cora was handing out biscuits with thin slices of antelope steak. When Michael approached he said, "Reuben, you and me got scout duty after we eat."

Reuben nodded and asked, "They see anything excitin'?"

"Nothin' but tracks. They seemed to think it was a bear, but they said it was bigger'n any tracks they ever saw before, and different somehow."

"But just tracks?"

"Yeah, just tracks." He walked toward the brush and asked Rachel if he could sit down, and her smile was all the answer he needed.

Cora offered, "Biscuit?"

"No thanks, ma'am. I got me some cornbread and jerky. Thanks anyway."

Cora nodded her head and sat down next to Reuben, looking at Rachel with one of those motherly looks that says, "Watch yourself." Reuben grinned and chuckled to himself, knowing what his mother meant with those stern looks.

REUBEN WAS PROUD OF HIS KILL. THE BIG MULE DEER BUCK was still in the velvet when he jumped from the oak brush startling Reuben and his horse, but the young man quickly gained control and slipped his Hawken from the scabbard and jumped to the ground to snap off a running shot and drop the big deer. When he saw it fall end over end, he was so elated he jumped in the air, again spooking his horse and he had to run after it so he wouldn't be left afoot. He was on his knees before the carcass, knife in hand, as he split the hide open from gullet to gonads. The guts spilled onto the grass in a puff of internal heat that emitted a thin cloud of steam. He turned his attention to the legs, severing them at the knee joint and casting the ends aside. He looked at the head, knowing it was to be severed as well, but he took in the size of the rack and knew this buck would have had a massive set of antlers had he been allowed to grow them to their max.

He hobbled to the neck and before he plunged the knife in, he arched his back and lifted his eyes to the trees beyond the brush littered dry creek bottom. Something moved! He reached for his Hawken that rested on the rump of the deer and remembered that in his excitement at dropping the buck, he had forgotten to reload. But he brought the rifle to his side without taking his eyes from the trees, and more movement captured his attention. Then he saw two mounted riders, Indians, moving uphill and away, picking their way through the dense trees and moving noiselessly. Within a moment, they disappeared over a ridge and into the ravine beyond. Reuben waited, repeatedly scanning the entire hillside, and reloaded his Hawken by feel rather than sight, not wanting to miss any movement that could foretell danger.

The clatter of hooves behind him made him turn quickly, rifle in hand, but he was relieved to see Michael Garmin approaching.

"Hey, I heard the shot. Nice deer!" he commented as he dropped to the ground to join his fellow scout.

"Didchu see 'em?" asked Reuben, quietly, as he turned to look again at the hillside.

"See who? Were there more deer in this bunch?" asked Michael, walking to his side.

"No. The Indians!" answered Reuben without turning to Michael, still searching the trees.

Michael dropped to the side of his friend and looked where he looked and asked, "No, I didn't see any Indians. How many?"

"Only two that I saw. I'm sure they saw me, probably heard my shot like you did. I was guttin' the deer, looked up and they moved back and took off. Up thataway," he added as he pointed to the finger ridge beyond.

"Well, it sure wouldn't be smart to follow 'em and we're close to two miles ahead of the train, and they should be toppin' out after that switchback." He lifted his eyes to the sun, "It's gettin' late so we probably oughta head back and let 'em know 'bout the Indians."

"Yeah, lemme finish with this an' you can help me load him. I was gonna take the whole thing, but let's just debone it and put the meat in the hide. It won't take the two of us very long and both our families can use the meat."

As expected, when the scouts returned to the wagons, the train was topping out above the switchbacks and George Garmin called for a stop to let the animals have a breather after the long uphill climb. When he saw the two scouts returning, he reined his mount around and moved to intercept them.

"Well, looks like you got yourselves some fresh meat!" he greeted.

"But we saw sumpin' else," declared Michael, looking to Reuben.

"Yeah, two Indians, and they saw me, but hightailed it into the trees an' up toward that long ridge yonder," he twisted in his saddle to point to the long timber covered ridge that rose more than twice the height of the nearby mountains beside the trail.

"Only two?" asked Garmin, visibly shaken.

"That's all. I kept watchin' the trees and didn't see any other movement. An' when Michael joined me, we both searched the hillside best we could, and didn't see anythin' else."

"Were they armed? Painted?"

"Couldn't tell, trees were too thick, but there was no mistakin' they was Indians."

Garmin looked around, "This is no place to camp, not enough room. How's it look up ahead?"

Michael spoke up, and turned in his saddle to point, "A little over two miles, there's a great place. Big, open flat, stream, an' you can see the valley from there!"

"But we have to go past the place where you saw the Indians?"

"Uh, yeah, but not too far."

"You two wait here. Since we're stopped anyway, I'll bring the others up here an' we'll decide together." He reined around and took off back to the wagons without waiting for a response.

Reuben looked at Michael and they both shrugged their shoulders and stepped down and walked to the slight slope north of the trail and seated themselves on the gravelly bank.

———

THE TEMPORARY CAMP of the Comanche village was in a basin with several small spring fed streams. The scouts were returning with their reports and Raven was pleased to hear the buffalo herd was moving as expected. He knew this land well and he had anticipated making their hunt as the herd approached and crossed the Sangre de Cristo Creek. He had planned well, and the hunters would be in position well before the herd's arrival. He looked up to see Fat Porcupine and Big Wolf riding towards his fire. The two men slid to the ground and Wolf began, "We saw wagons, this many!" he held both hands with all fingers extended, "and it is possible the scouts for the wagon saw us. We were surprised when the one scout shot a deer that ran toward the trees where we were."

Raven stood to look at the scouts, "Did the scout shoot at you?"

"No, he was gutting the deer when he saw us, and we took to the thick timber."

"The wagons, freighters or families?"

"Families, many women and children. Mebbe three hands of men."

"Where will they camp?"

"The flats atop the pass where the creeks join."

Raven nodded his head and dismissed the scouts. He considered the reports, and his primary concern was to have a successful buffalo hunt, but the easy target of ten wagons and the bounty of rifles and other goods was also tempting. A warrior at heart, his blood sought battle, but he could not sacrifice the need for meat for the people and everything the buffalo herd could supply. And with the rest of the village, women and children at risk, they could not chance an attack on the wagons. He also knew some of the young warriors might choose the wagons for the honors they would gain with a successful attack, but the attack could also endanger the village and he could not allow them that privilege that would otherwise be theirs to choose. But, if the wagons interfered with their hunt, that must also be considered. He must call a council of the leaders and decide together. If he alone tried to restrict the young warriors, they could ignore his demand and face no consequences, but if the council made that decision, everyone must abide by their decree.

Big Wolf was the most expressive of the young warriors as he voiced the will of the generation of warriors that had few opportunities to gain the honors as had the older men. To fight the whites, and take captives and weapons brought great honor to any successful warriors and the scalps and battle scars were displayed with pride. Young men that sought to take a woman as a mate would have to pay a bride price and that could only be gained from raids on the enemy.

But the quiet voices of the proven warriors and elders outweighed the enthusiastic entreaties of the young, and the council chose to demand the young men avoid the wagons and gain their honors with a successful hunt. One of the respected leaders, the war chief Antelope Horn, vowed to take the young warriors on a raid to the south against the farmers in the Rio Grande Valley, where they could do battle and steal horses to buy their brides. This promise was met with shouts and war cries from the anxious warriors and all vowed to have a great hunt.

Raven stood to signify the end of the council and the men filed from his lodge. He tapped Antelope Horn and motioned for him to wait. When the lodge was emptied, Raven and Horn sat back down, and Raven started, "Big Wolf is still angry he could not go against the whites. I ask you to take him and some others with you tomorrow to watch the wagons. Do not attack, as that is against the will of the council, but we must know the whites of the wagons will not endanger our hunt. I believe they will leave at first light and that would put them into the valley after the sun is at its highest. It would be better if they were there sooner, and before the buffalo are near. I believe they will go north in the valley and that would take them away from the buffalo, or if they go west also. But they must go early."

Antelope Horn looked at his chief and dropped his head as he began to grin. He lifted his face back to Raven, a broad smile showing, and he laughed. "What you ask is to teach these young warriors how to fight without fighting. It will also show them how brave or not so brave these white men are, is this true?"

Raven looked at Antelope and fought a grin as he forced a straight face, "I did not say that. I only ask you to watch the wagons to keep them from our hunt."

Antelope chuckled, stood and said, "I will do as my chief asks." The men clasped forearms and Antelope ducked to make his way from the lodge. It was by the remaining moonlight, as the golden orb hung in the western sky, that the village started the last of their trek to the valley and their anticipated buffalo hunt. Antelope led the way with eight young warriors following.

———

THE WAGONS HAD BEEN PULLED into a tight circle with the tongue of one under the tailgate of the other. All the animals, after being watered and grazed, were contained within the circle. Throughout the night, there were at least four men on guard and diligently walking the perimeter of the wagons. With two-hour shifts, every able-bodied man served his time on guard. Although it was a peaceful night, several of the men were alarmed whenever a nighthawk cried or the cicadas quieted, and when their shift was over, they gladly turned into their bedrolls.

Garmin and Greene were part of the last shift and stopped to talk to one another as the first hint of grey began to show in the east.

"I was wishin' we still had Bent with us, he knows the Indians and how to deal with 'em. This is the first time we had to make the decision about defendin' against an attack," grumbled Garmin.

"I know whatchu mean. I was wishin' we'd made it to the flats where we could see 'em comin' if they did. What're we gonna do if they attack while we're stretched out on the trail?"

"All we can do is try to run. At least it's downhill an' the mules can mebbe get us outta harm's way. Mebbe . . . " he paused as he thought a moment, "Mebbe we need to tell the men to have their weapons ready an' if the Injuns come, they could either have their women get in the back o' the wagon and do the shootin' or they could have them drive while they shoot. Whaddaya think?"

"Well, we can give 'em a choice, let them decide. But, we need to be ready anyway, cuz, what I seen o' that road yonder, there ain't gonna be no place to circle the wagons an' try to fight 'em off if'n they do attack," answered Greene.

"It's gonna be light soon, let's roust 'em out and get an early start. Mebbe we'll get outta these mountains 'fore the Injuns even get outta their bedrolls," replied Garmin, hopefully.

———

ANTELOPE HORN LED his braves over the timbered ridge and down to the hills that overlooked the wide valley and the roadway. He reminded them of the council's restrictions and explained the actions they were to take. With his knowledge of the area and the lay of the land, he had chosen the position for each of his warriors well, providing them with visibility of the road and protection afforded by either the juniper and piñon, or the contour of the land. They were to be seen, but not endangered. As they rode over the hilltops, he stationed the men near the bald clearings and above the road. His eight warriors were in position by the first light of morning, and each anxiously awaited.

———

NO ONE WAITED for biscuits or cornbread for breakfast. They kindled small fires for coffee, and weak coffee at that. Everyone was a touch on the nervous side, trying to pierce the darkness with their sidelong glances, fearful of seeing a horde of blood-thirsty Indians coming at them. The mule teams were hitched, wagons lined out and scouts sent ahead in record time. Garmin didn't let loose his usual holler to start the train, just lifted his arm and waved as he dropped it forward. The rattle of trace chains, the squeak of axles and wheels, and the slap of lines told of the movement. It was no more than fifty yards to the trail and the crest of the pass, and it would be a downhill grade from there. The sun was just appearing over their left shoulders as the train stretched out. Spears of gold pierced the pink clouds as the mountains caught the glow on their granite peaks. It was a beautiful morning, but those in the wagon weren't enamored with the beauty around them but were troubled by the fear that churned in their bellies.

The women and children that would often walk behind the wagons were all sheltered within the white canvas bonnets and the men cracked whips and snapped lines to the rumps of sleepy eyed mules. Because of the threat of an Indian attack, the captains had assigned the scouts to cover all sides. Alfred Hays and Hank Greene were taking their turn in the lead well ahead of the wagons, and the Honeycutt brothers, Matthew and Luke, were on drag behind the train.

The captains wanted the two scouts that had spotted the Indians the day before to take the flanks, as they were certain if an attack came, it would be from the sides. Michael Garmin was on the right and Reuben was on the left. They had no trail to follow and their course was the most difficult and often forced them to ride close to the wagons, but they kept their eyes on the hillsides around them. Reuben moved through the brush and across the Sangre de Cristo Creek, so he could see into the black timber that rose on the south facing slopes. He dropped to the ground and walked, trailing his mount behind as he often bent low to peer into the thick trees. He would stop and listen, and as Bent had told him, wait to hear the woods breathe. The whisper of the morning breeze carried the chatter of chipmunks, the melodious songs of the meadowlarks; the sounds let Reuben breathe as well. Nothing was stirring in the woods and he mounted up and trotted along the tree line, as he glanced across the creek to the wagons.

The train moved at a good pace, the only noise that of trace chains and the squeal of brake pads on the metal rim of the wheels. It was as much work for the mules to hold the wagons back as it was to drag them up a hill. But with the men focused on the wagons and the teams, they had little time to worry about Indians. Reuben saw Michael moving across the face of a gravelly slope above the road, his horse was working at finding footing as Michael searched the hillside above him. He shaded his eyes from the morning sun and looked across the narrow valley to see Reuben by the tree line, in the shade and lifting an easy wave to his friend. The train had made about four miles when the trees on both sides began to thin out and give way to lower hills covered with sage, cactus and dotted with clusters of juniper and piñon.

Reuben had worked his way forward until he was almost at the front of the train when he looked down the road and saw Alfred Mays and Hank Greene coming back at a gallop, laying low on their horses' necks and waving hats in the air. George Garmin's wagon was in the lead and he drew up to hear the report. Mays pulled his horse to a stop beside the wagon seat, and yelled, "Indians! Lots of 'em!" he twisted in his saddle to point to the south side of the road and the hills beyond, "Up on the tops o' them hills. They was screamin' and yellin', wavin' their lances an' such, and gettin' ready to come attack!"

———

Big Wolf was snoozing under the low branches of a juniper when Running Buffalo kicked his moccasined foot to rouse him. The man came up suddenly with his war club in hand, ready to do battle. Running Buffalo stopped him with a soft word, "Wagons!"

Wolf swung aboard his mount and rode to his assigned position. Buffalo walked his horse to his overlook to await the wagons. Within moments, the wagons were on the road below and Big Wolf began yelling his war cry and pumping his lance in the air, making his horse rear up and paw the sky with his hooves, wanting to be certain the people of the wagons saw him. He knew they would look, but they would also search the skyline and see the others and think there were more. Shortly after Wolf started his antics, Running Buffalo was true to his name and ran his horse from one side of the clearing to the other, screaming and shouting and waving his war club in the air. Each of the warriors were attired in their war paraphernalia, feathers and fringe that showed exaggerated each move. Buffalo brought his horse to a sudden halt and nocked an arrow and sent it flying in a high arch to impale itself in the side of the lead wagon. He laughed when he saw the reaction of the people below and shouted more war cries and dropped to the uphill side of his horse and ran it back to the cluster of juniper.

He heard Wolf shouting and screaming as his horse was kicking up the gravelly hillside and they both watched as the men of the wagons shouted and slapped their lines and cracked their whips to start the mule teams running. They heard women screaming, mules braying, and men shouting, and Big Wolf trotted his horse along the hilltop toward Running Buffalo. When he came to Buffalo's side, they both shouted and between war cries, they laughed and mocked the cowardly white men.

———

Garmin could only think of the conversation he had with Harold Greene earlier, when they had agreed their only hope would be to run. He hollered back at the scared scout, "Go! Tell the others to stretch 'em out. Our only hope is to try'n outrun 'em! Go!" He dropped back into his seat and lifted his whip and hollered, "Heeeyawww!" and cracked the whip over the heads of the mules. The animals surged into their collars and harness, kicking gravel with their hooves, and the wagon rocked back as the trace chains pulled taut and the wagon was on its way. The others had seen the scouts alarm, and with the shout and whip crack of the lead wagon, they quickly responded with shouts of alarm and slaps of reins and the wagons seemed to surge together and quickly began to pick up speed. The men were leaning forward in their seats, one foot on the brake lever, both hands full of lines as they sought to guide the animals aright. The dust rose behind each wagon as they bounced over the uneven trail. The grass lined ridge in the middle of the wheel ruts soon disappeared in the dirt; women were heard screaming and the men shouted at the mules. The rattles of sideboards and tailgates compounded the confusion and cacophony of fear.

Reuben reined around and gigged his mount toward the rear of the train where his family wagon was next to the last in the line. As the other wagons surged forward, he saw rather than heard his mother stand and crack the whip and he knew she was yelling at the top of her hoarse voice, calling each of the mules by their not so flattering names. "Move out you flop eared cayuses, git up there you graygrey humpbacks, on with you Scratch! Move out Flea-Bit, hyaah with you Uglier'n Me, pull you worthless Line Back!"

Even with the excitement and fear of their lives, Reuben couldn't keep from laughing at his mother's antics. He jerked his horse alongside the leader and bent to grab the side of its headstall and shouted, "Move it!" He tugged at the leather strap, and when the mule leaned into his collar, Reuben doffed his hat and used it to slap the rump of the left wheel mule as he pulled alongside. The wagon rocked as the mules finally decided to pull as the line-handler demanded, and the wagon moved faster.

———

As THE WAGONS picked up the pace on the downhill slope, the

other warriors repeated the actions of Buffalo and Wolf. Each one shouting their own war cries and screaming as they ran their horses back and forth across the clearings. They reveled in their actions exposing what they saw as the cowardice of the white men.

With random glances to the ridges, the people of the wagons saw the continual action of the Indians as the actions of many. As they imagined great numbers of attackers and their panic in their flight, their fear and terror were multiplied with each sighting. Men that had thought of themselves as brave and even fearful were showing themselves cowardly as they screamed at the mules and mercilessly brought their whips to bear.

The warriors were greatly entertained by the frantic actions of the white men. It was all they could do to keep up the charade as they found it difficult to sound fierce and mean when all they wanted to do was laugh. But they did all they could to hasten the white men on their way and with each sighting, the wagons seemed to move faster.

By the time the wagons passed the last of the warriors, the men of the Comanche village were returning to give their report to their leader. Antelope waited for each one's return. He was pleased with the reports and laughed with each one as they told their tales of the fleeing wagons.

———

THE RITTER WAGON was about twenty yards behind the wagon of the bully-in-the-making Sidney Northrup and about the same distance ahead of the bookkeeper and his wife, Frank and Mildred Simpson. Cora could hear the screams of Mildred and the whining answer of her husband as they did their best to keep up. With the dust of eight wagons in front of them, Cora struggled to see the road and pulled her neckerchief up around her nose and mouth, quickly sorting out the reins to two-hand them again. She squinted and ducked and bobbed her head, trying to see through the dust and was forced to lean back and slow the team to back away from the wagon before her.

When she slowed, she heard the screams from behind her and hollered to Reuben, "Check on them," nodding her head to the rear, "and get her to stop her consarned screaming!"

Reuben reined up and waited for the last wagon, moved alongside and hollered, "Everything alright?"

"Yeah! Where's the Indians?" asked the bookkeeper, with wide white eyes as he ducked the slaps of his wife.

"Nevermind them, just drive!" demanded the overbearing woman.

Reuben kicked his heels into the ribs of his horse and the animal leaped forward, digging hooves into the rough gravelly dirt beside the trail. The horse slipped, and Reuben pulled a taut rein that helped the animal regain his balance, and they moved beside the Ritter wagon at a run. He hollered to his ma, "They're alright! Keep goin'!" and waved his mother forward. He turned away from the trail to the creek bottom, riding in the grass beside the creek and willows. He gained on the other wagons, saw no sign of Indian attack and went back beside the family wagon. The sounds of the running teams and rattling wagons filled the widening valley and the dust cloud obscured the vision of the hillsides. Reuben had a quick thought that there could be hundreds of Indians a few hundred yards away and he wouldn't see them because of the dust. Even if they were attacking and shooting and screaming their war cries, they wouldn't be heard because of the stampeding wagons.

The trail took a turn to the left and the wagons slid and bounced around the bend, straightened out and stretched out again, only to see a wide bend to the right. The valley was broad, the hills low and sparsely covered when the dust thinned making it possible to see the trail. The lead wagon took the curve easily, the captain leaning into the task and whipping the mules to stretch out on the long straight slope that promised the wide San Luis Valley below. Each wagon slowed for the first curve but stretched out after the second. As the wagons took the curves to follow those before them, men were yelling and women screaming as the mules lathered up and fought the harnesses. As the Ritter wagon came to the tight left-hand curve it slid around the bend, but the rear wheel dropped into a rut and something cracked like a rifle shot! The wagon box dropped, and the back end dragged pulling the wagon down. Cora leaned back against the reins, bracing her feet against the edge of the wagon box struggling to pull the running mules to the side of the trail. Once stopped, she shouted and motioned for the wagon behind to come up. She was jumping down on the far side when the Simpsons came alongside and slowed. Simpson yelled in his squeaky voice, "Your axle's broke! We'll tell the others!" and slapped the reins to his mules and took off into the dust cloud.

Cora stood with her hands on her hips as she watched the last wagon disappear around the far bend, then quickly said, "Rachel, get your rifle ready, I'm gonna check the wagon," and ran to the back to look at the cause of their breakdown. She didn't have to look hard, it was evident the rear axle was indeed broken, the left wheel sat at an angle, and the other wheel lay on the ground, three spokes broken. She knew they had a spare wheel, but not a spare axle. She looked around and as the dust cleared, she saw two mounted Indians, watching them from atop the hill beyond the creek. They weren't moving, just watching. She spoke softly, "Rachel, there's two Indians atop that hill to yore left, yonder. They're within range of your Sharps but don't shoot unless they come down, understand?"

"Yeah Ma, I see 'em. I got 'em in my sights."

Cora walked back to the front of the wagon and stood in the middle of the trail looking to see if there were any wagons still in sight. As she looked, a horseman came at a run from below the road and near the creek, and she recognized Reuben. He had ridden forward as the flank scout to watch for any attack, but when the family wagon didn't come, he came at a run to help. He was riding low at a gallop and pointed his horse to the trail which lay above the creek bottom and on the slight shoulder of the mountain. As the horse turned toward the trail, suddenly the horse's head dropped between his front feet and the animal flipped end over end, launching Reuben into an arc over his head to land in a heap beside a cluster of prickly pear cactus. Cora gasped at the sight and screamed, "Nooo!" and started running toward her son. She yelled over her shoulder, "Stay there, Rachel!"

CHAPTER EIGHTEEN

BROKEN

Big Wolf and Running Buffalo watched the wagons racing down the roadway, stirring up enough of a dust cloud to blanket the entire valley bottom. Big Wolf was grinning and pointing as both of them laughed at the white men that were so scared they were whipping the teams into a heavy lather in their bid to escape an attack that would not come.

"Antelope Horn was right. All we had to do was look like we were attacking, and they would flee for their lives," said Running Buffalo. "It is a good thing to learn."

"Yes, but I would rather be taking scalps than watching the cowardly whites run!" answered Big Wolf.

Buffalo reined his mount around and said, "We are to tell Raven what we see, and I know our shaman, White Feather also wants to hear."

Big Wolf took one last look and started to follow, "Wait! Look, one has stopped!"

Buffalo turned back to look and saw the last wagon pass the one that appeared to have been damaged. They watched, surprised that the others would leave one behind without helping. Buffalo nudged Wolf and pointed to the rider that was returning. When the horse stumbled and fell, they saw the rider fly through the air and land near the cactus, and both winced at what they knew the rider must have felt. They watched as the one from the wagon started to help,

"That is a woman!" said Big Wolf.

"Look at the wagon. That is another woman, but she has her rifle pointed at us!"

"We could take them and have captives and a scalp and rifles!" suggested Big Wolf anxiously, still hoping for anything that would give him honors.

"No! The council has made it clear, we cannot attack! If we do, anything we would take would be taken from us and there would be no honor," reminded Buffalo. He turned away and started through the trees, with a reluctant and somewhat angry Big Wolf following.

RAVEN AND WHITE Feather rode at the front of the caravan of villagers, Raven showing nothing that would tell of his position as chief other than three notched and painted feathers at the back of his head. A shaman would customarily have the skull cap of a buffalo as a headdress, but White Feather had fashioned a beaded headband with the tips of two buffalo horns at the sides that told of her position, as did the rest of her regalia, beaded armbands, tunic with porcupine quills and beads in a pattern that matched both moccasins and leggings. She was a respected leader and well known among the Comanche and other tribes for her healing skills.

Antelope Horn had instructed his warriors to report back to their chief after the wagons had passed their position. When Running Buffalo and Big Wolf returned to the caravan at a canter, they were the first to report.

"Ho, my chief! The wagons have run and will soon be in the valley!" declared Wolf.

"Yes, but they left one behind. Two women and one man, maybe," added Buffalo.

"Maybe?" asked Raven.

"Yes, a man came to help those of the wagon, but his horse fell, and he was thrown. It was a bad fall and he did not move," explained Wolf.

"And the other wagons, they did not stop or return?" asked Raven, confused.

"No, one passed the wagon by without stopping and they all kept running. No others came back," explained Buffalo, looking at his shaman, White Feather. "The one that fell, did not move, but I could tell he was hurt, perhaps in need of healing."

White Feather turned to Raven, "I will go see these that have been left. It would be good to be of help."

"You do not know these white men, they will try to kill you!" warned Raven.

"I must see them before I decide," declared White Feather.

When she started away, Raven shook his head and gigged his horse to catch up to her and accompany his sister that he had vowed to his father to always protect. "You are more stubborn than an old bull buffalo!" White Feather looked to her brother and smiled, for this was a familiar argument and he never won.

It was just a few moments and they sat on the bald knob above the roadway and looked down at the wagon and the white people. The man that had been thrown was still down, with a woman at his side, and the other woman still sat in the wagon, watching. White Feather led as she and Raven and Running Buffalo started toward the wagon.

"Ma! Ma! There's Indians coming!"

Cora turned away from her son and looked to where

Rachel was pointing and saw three mounted Indians slowly riding toward them.

"Do I shoot?" asked Rachel, nervously, as she propped her foot on the wagon sideboard and rested the muzzle of the Sharps on her knee.

"No, not unless it looks like they wanna shoot us," answered Cora as she slowly stood to watch them approach. She thought one of them looked like a woman, but she wasn't sure, as she stood with hands on hips, waiting.

White Feather rode to the two that were below the road and away from the wagon. The man on the ground appeared to be unconscious and the woman that stood over him protectively looked wary. White Feather slid from her horse and turned to the woman, "Is he your man?"

"He's my son," answered Cora, surprised to be talking to an Indian in English.

"What is his name?"

"Reuben, and my daughter yonder is Rachel. They are twins."

White Feather looked at the woman and let a slow smile paint her face and said, "It is an honor to be the mother of twins."

"I think so," answered Cora, frowning at this Indian woman.

"I am a Shaman among my people, may I look at your son?"

Cora just waved a hand toward Reuben and knelt on one knee beside him. White Feather also knelt beside the young man and saw a few scrapes on his face, a rising knot on his head, nothing bleeding, and as her eyes traveled down his body, she saw blood on his pants leg and that the leg was bent at an awkward angle. She slipped a big Bowie knife from its scabbard and bent toward his leg but was stopped by Cora, "What're you gonna do?"

"His leg is broken, and he is bleeding. I will cut his pants to see to his leg," explained White Feather, patiently, but without pausing in her actions. The razor-sharp blade made short work of splitting the pants leg and she heard a gasp from Cora as the wound was revealed. A sharp edge of the bone was protruding from the skin, blood came from the open tear and White Feather motioned for Running Buffalo to join her. She flipped the knife and held it by the blade, extending it to Cora. "Go to the willows and cut many straight branches, at least as big as your thumb or bigger, we will need them to support his leg." Cora looked at the woman, paused a moment as she considered her actions, then took the knife and trotted to the willows to busy herself with the cutting.

White Feather waved her brother over to help, sent Running Buffalo back to the horses for her saddle bags, and prepared to work on Reuben's leg.

"You sit down at his head and hold his shoulders. I must set the bone and you will have to hold him. Give me your knife," she instructed Raven, and he tossed it haft first to her. Buffalo returned with her pack and set it down beside her, flipping open the flap for her access. To Buffalo she said, "I will need to cut the flesh to see the bone, make a poultice as I showed you, and use the buckskin to hold it in place."

She probed the break, feeling for the end of the bone under the skin, looked carefully at the protruding bone, and made a T shaped cut, exposing the area to reveal the area for the joining of the ends. Cora had returned, dropping the willow sticks to the side as she knelt down beside Reuben. She looked at the cut made by the shaman, lifted her eyes to the woman and scowled, but said nothing. Blood flowed freely, but Feather ignored it as she instructed Raven, "We will turn him on his side, then I will pull to set the bones."

Both Raven and Feather rolled Reuben to his uninjured

side, prompting Cora to move back. When Reuben was settled, Feather put her right foot to Reuben's buttock, her left foot at his crotch, and his leg in her lap. She nodded to Raven and began to pull on Reuben's ankle while watching the movement of the bones. After considerable struggle, the exposed bone slid into the cut-away area and Feather saw the joining of the two ends. Cora was kneeling beside her son and holding her breath as the two worked on his leg. Fortunately, the break was not too jagged, and the bone ends seemed to fit together nicely. Feather slowly released pressure and nodded to Buffalo to hold the poultice against the wound.

Feather stood and stretched, arching her back to release the tension, and knelt beside the leg. She reached back into her bags and brought out some thin twisted sinew and a needle. Reuben was still on his side with Raven holding his shoulders, and as White Feather moved the leg slightly, Reuben moaned, but did not come awake. The woman began stitching the wound together, daubing at the blood as she worked, and soon had the wound closed and the bleeding mostly stopped. She spoke to Buffalo, "Make up another poultice and wrap the leg well with wide buckskin. We will put the willow on and strap them tight."

Cora had watched all that White Feather did and was amazed at the skill of the woman. She knew the work was as good as any white doctor would have done, perhaps even better. She looked at White Feather and asked, "Where did you learn to do this?"

White Feather smiled and said, "My people have done these things always. My skill is learned from those that have gone before me."

"Well, I'm mighty beholden to you. What now?" asked Cora, thinking not only of her son but their predicament and the presence of the Indians that she didn't understand.

"Your people have left you behind. What do you want to do?" asked Feather.

"Well, the wagon's busted and can't be fixed. But I've got strong mules and can load muh stuff on them and keep on goin', I reckon. William Bent said there was a man around these parts name o' Tate Saint, and Bent said he might get us goin' in the right direction."

Feather's eyes widened when she heard the name of her friend, and she stood to look at the woman and over at her wagon. "Load your mules and we will make a travois for your son, I will take you to the lodge of this man Tate Saint."

Cora looked at Feather, surprise written on her face, and turned to the wagon to unhitch and load the mules with their gear. Rachel climbed from the wagon box as her mother neared, "Is he alright?"

"I think so, that woman's a shaman, I think that's like a medicine man or something, and she fixed him up purty good. Prob'ly couldn't a' done better with a sawbones." Cora was digging her gear from the wagon as she talked. "We're gonna go with her, she said she knows this Saint fella an' will get us to his cabin.

"What if somebody from the wagons come back?"

Cora stopped what she was doing and looked at Rachel, "You mean, what if Michael comes back?"

"Yeah, I was hopin' he would."

"Well, it's a good thing he didn't. I think them Indians over there woulda done him in if he had."

"But surely, somebody would come back to help?" pleaded the girl.

Cora stopped again, turning to face Rachel with one hand on her hip and the other on the wagon box, "Look, they probably think we done been kilt by the Injuns an' figger they couldn't help none if they did come back. Most o' them men ain't got much of a backbone as it is an' they're prob'ly glad to be shut of us. They didn't like havin' a wagon with no man along. So, just put them outta your mind and let's get this gear packed so we can get outta here."

Rachel was surprised and disappointed in her mother's response, and didn't want to admit she was probably right. She turned back to the task with lingering thoughts of Michael on her mind.

Raven reined away from the wagon after giving his sister a cautionary word. "You will probably be needed after the hunt. There are often those that are injured when they ride among the buffalo."

"Yes, and Running Buffalo has shown his skills with those injuries. I believe he could do what is needed. But if I am needed, you will know where I may be found," answered White Feather. She and her brother had been friends with Tate Saint since his first year in the mountains and he had helped their people overcome a smallpox epidemic. Had he not been there with his knowledge, the entire village could have died, but he selflessly helped them and taught them what to do with the sick and the dying. White Feather was his translator and the two had grown close during that time. Had she not been chosen to be the next shaman she and Tate might have become mates. But their friendship had grown through the years and they respected one another, and Tate's woman and White Feather had become great friends.

It had been at least two summers since they last visited and White Feather was anxious to see her friends and was thinking about them when Cora asked, "Did I hear you and your brother say something about a buffalo hunt?"

"Yes, our people are following a great herd and they will start the hunt tomorrow. The herd will be in the valley below."

Cora thought about it and asked, "Would it be helpful if we could shoot some buffalo for your people?"

White Feather frowned as she looked at this woman that was almost a head shorter than Feather and asked, "Who would do this shooting? Your son is not able to shoot."

Cora chuckled at her response and answered, "Rachel there," nodding toward her daughter, "and me, are pretty handy with our rifles. And we have rifles that can shoot very far and can bring down a buffalo with one bullet." Cora smiled and looked to the skeptical Shaman.

"What do you mean by far?"

Cora looked around and picked out a rocky shoulder on the hillside beyond the creek, about seven hundred yards distant. She pointed, "See them rocks yonder?"

Feather looked where Cora pointed and back at the woman, "There is no rifle that can shoot that far, and then kill a buffalo."

"Would you like me to show you?" asked Cora, reining the mule to a stop.

"Yes, I would see this rifle that can shoot that far," answered the doubtful Feather. She brought her horse to a stop and slipped to the ground. The travois was behind her mount as the mules weren't very accepting of the rig behind them and kept kicking at it, so Feather had volunteered her experienced horse. She held the headstall of the horse and watched as Cora slipped her Sharps from the scabbard. The woman dropped to one knee on the edge of the trail and used her knee to rest her elbow and sighted the rifle on the rocks. "That round one sittin' on the top o' the stack," she said, selecting her target so there would be no doubt. She eared back the hammer, setting the trigger, took in a deep breath, let part of it out and slowly squeezed the front trigger. When the blast from the rifle sounded, it echoed across the valley and the grey smoke spewed from the muzzle, the round rock exploded when the .52 caliber lead missile struck. As the report seemed to echo down the valley, all else was silent and no one moved for a moment until Feather said, "Aiiieee, that is truly a shoots far rifle!"

Cora smiled and stood up with the rifle at her side. "And it doesn't just shoot far, it can also shoot fast! For every time a man can shoot a Hawken rifle, I can shoot mine six or eight times! And my daughter there, why, she can shoot ever bit as good as I can!"

Feather looked at the woman with wonder and turned back to her horse to mount up. Cora slipped her rifle into the scabbard and stepped aboard the mule and looked at Feather, "So, do you think I could be of help? Now, mind you, I don't wanna interfere, but you've already done so much for us, I just thought mebbe that might be a help to your people."

"Yes, I see what you mean. We will meet up with my people soon, and I will ask our chief. Most of our meat for the winter will be taken in this hunt. And the hides and more are all important to our people. Because of this, I do not know what he will say."

"This chief, is he a hard man?" asked Cora, wondering about these people and picturing a chief with a massive war bonnet and grey hair and a wrinkled face that showed his age.

"No, he is a good man. He is my brother, Raven. He was with me when we came to you."

"Him? He's your chief? Why, he don't look old enough to be a chief."

Feather laughed and asked, "And just how old does a man have to be to lead others?"

Cora shook her head at her own foolishness and answered, "I'm sorry, I just thought of a chief as an old man. Guess I was wrong."

IT WAS LESS than two miles farther down the road where Wagon Creek joined the Sangre de Cristo creek and the valleys merged. The caravan of Comanche was already at the confluence of the streams and starting down the trail toward the San Luis Valley. Raven saw his sister and the others coming and was waiting for them in the shade of a tall juniper. When they came near, he greeted them, "Ho! My sister and those from the wagons, I thought maybe you had become lost!"

"Ha! It is my brother that gets lost in the woods, not me!" she declared. It was a familiar greeting between the siblings and was met with the smiles of one another. "My brother, this woman, Cora, has asked if she could help with our buffalo hunt. She is a proven buffalo hunter and her rifle speaks loud and shoots far, farther than any of our warriors can shoot with their weapons!"

Raven turned his attention to the odd figure on the mule and looked back at his sister with a questioning expression, thinking his sister might be joking him. But Feather added, "I have seen her shoot and she shot a rock this size," she held her hands about a foot and a half apart, "and it was so far away, it was hard to see." She looked across the valley and said, "It was as far as that lone tree on the hillside!" and pointed to a lone cedar tree half way up the hill beyond the creek, a distance of about six hundred yards.

"Ha! You must be wrong, there is no rifle that can shoot that far!" declared the experienced and proud leader.

Feather laughed and looked to Cora, nodding her head. Feather grinned at the skepticism of her brother and watched as Cora slipped the Sharps from the scabbard and stepped down from the mule and walked to the side of the road. She repeated her shot from before and the horse of Raven shied away at the loud report and the many villagers that were walking on the far trail stopped and looked. Cora had chosen a rock beside the tree and it had shattered at the impact of the bullet. Raven was even more impressed than Feather as he looked at the woman that wasn't much taller than her rifle. He looked at his sister and Feather said, "And that one," pointing at Rachel, "can do the same with her rifle!"

The explosion from the Sharps caught the attention of several of the warriors that rode to the side of their chief to see what was happening. They listened and looked, each one also amazed as Cora casually walked back to her mule and slipped the rifle into the scabbard. She mounted up and looked at Raven, "If I can be of help, I would be glad to, your sister has done so much for us already, it would be the least we could do, but only if you say it would be alright. I ain't wantin' to interfere or nuthin, just help out."

Raven looked at the woman, at the girl, and back at the woman. "To have more buffalo is a good thing, but you might shame some of my warriors. I will let you know." He reined his horse around and trotted back to the lead of the caravan, followed by all the curious warriors that were chattering among themselves.

Cora chuckled and said to Feather, "Ain't men all alike? They just can't stand a woman that can do what they do only better!"

"It is so with our people as well. Many times, I have had to show my brother where he is wrong, but it must always be proven to him, and even then, he finds it hard to, how you say, swallow his pride!" Feather chuckled at the remembrance of the many times the siblings had quarreled, always good naturedly, but most often she was in the right and her brother was humbled. She looked to the white woman with respect and she knew the woman was much wiser than she originally thought her to be, and she also knew she would be a good friend.

IT WAS THE GREENER GRASS THAT BROUGHT THE HERD CLOSER to the mountains. With the runoff from winter snows and the spring rains, the wide flats below the foothills were green with buffalo grass, blue grama, and bunchgrass. The scattered patches of sage and cholla were crowded out with the plentiful grasses. As the buffalo moved north, they naturally followed the green and for the Comanche, it was a familiar route and one they counted on for their hunt.

At the mouth of the valley of the Sangre de Cristo Creek, the villagers turned into a basin that provided cover and shelter from the winds off the wide San Luis Valley. A narrow row of hills shielded them from the valley and the path of the herd, and the people had camped here before for the seasonal hunts. White Feather led the Ritter family to a site near the one selected by Running Buffalo for the tribe's Shaman.

"You may put your shelter here," motioned White Feather, "and your fire there. My lodge will be here, and we will scout the area for the hunt at dusk. If my brother says you may help, he will have a place for you. Your man is coming awake and I will bring you something for you to give him for his pain."

"Thanks Feather, you have been very good to us. I hope we can help your people with the hunt, cuz I shore don't know how else we can repay you," said Cora as she stepped down from the mule to start making their camp.

Feather looked at the woman, frowned, "Among my people, when one helps another, it is not to be repaid. But if you can do a kindness, then it is expected that you will do it."

"That's a good way to live. We can learn a lot from you and your people. Uh, White Feather, how far is it to the cabin of Tate Saint?"

"From here it is two days. The hunt will be after first light, and we can leave after. We will be at the cabin by the end of the second day."

THE SANGRE DE Cristo Ccreek bent to the south around the point of hills and meandered out into the flats of the valley. Raven rode with White Feather and Cora to scout out the shooters' locations and followed the north bank of the creek, shielded from the lower valley by the thick willows. When the willows thinned out, Raven pointed to the opposite bank, "Those with rifles will be there," he pointed to the brushy south bank, "the buffalo will come north, and the mounted hunters will come from that ridge." He nodded to the long cap rocked ridge that ran north and south bordering the narrow part of the green valley. Beyond the ridge the San Luis Valley stretched fifteen miles to the Rio Grande and another twenty miles beyond before bordered by the lower San Juan Mountains.

Before first light, Cora rolled from her bedroll and nudged Rachel awake. "We need to get to the creek 'fore them buffler do, so come on now," whispered Cora.

Rachel sat up and looked at her brother, still sleeping and she looked to her mother, "Will he be alright?"

"He'll prob'ly sleep through ever'thing. But he won't be goin' nowhere. That tea that Feather give him'll prob'ly help him sleep. But we won't be long. Feather said the others'll do the butcherin' and we can leave right away. So, come on," she urged as she stood with rifle in hand and possibles pouch hanging under her elbow.

Rachel pulled on her boots and stood to stomp her feet into them and followed her mother to the mules. They saddled two, mounted up and started for the creek. When they arrived at the creek bank, several Comanche were already positioning themselves and paid little attention to the women. Cora looked the area over, motioned for Rachel to follow and about fifteen yards away from the others, they tethered their mules where they would be well hidden in the willows and cottonwoods. The women slipped their rifles from the scabbards, took the bipods under arm, and walked away from the creek to a thick clump of sage that set back about twenty yards towards the hills and away from the other shooters.

They readied themselves and sat back to wait. Cora noticed the other shooters motioning toward them and laughing, and she had a pretty good idea what they were thinking. She smiled and motioned to Rachel, "Ain't they gonna be surprised?"

Rachel laughed with her mother, but the levity was soon stopped as they felt the ground begin to shake and they quickly came up to one knee and placed their bipods for their rifles and settled the muzzles on the v supports. With the sun barely showing grey across the sky, the herd was on the move. It wasn't because of a stampede that they felt the movement, but the sheer number of animals. With the valley between the far ridge and the hills behind being just over two miles wide, the herd easily covered half that distance. The brown tide was pushed by a rising dust cloud and the green valley floor disappeared beneath the carpet of beasts. The herd was moving slowly, grazing as they did, unalarmed and caring only for their graze.

Suddenly, every head of the wooly monsters of the plains lifted and the cries of the mounted hunters carried over the lowing rumble of the grunting buffalo. The herd began to move as one, the lead cows showing the way and they started at a rumbling trot, but the louder the cries of the Comanche hunters, the faster the brown wave came. The low hanging massive heads swung side to side, tongues lolling, the big black eyes encircled by white as the herd bulls pushed and prodded the rest to move at a run. The thundering hooves digging into the dusty adobe soil kicked dust clouds with every step, brown wooly hides became grey dusty blankets. Bellows, crashing horns, clattering hooves, and the screams of the mounted hunters filled the valley floor and the earth trembled.

When the herd neared, Cora could tell the animals were bound for the creek and her chosen position would be safe. She spoke to Rachel, "Pick your shots, we wanna drop 'em, not wound 'em. I figger mebbe three each'll be 'nuff."

"Sure Ma!"

Cora fired first, and the puff of dust was barely seen, but the bull nosed down and tumbled over. Rachel's first shot scored, and the women quickly reloaded, and in short order, the field before them had several carcasses that caused the herd to swerve. Cora said, "We done most of our shootin' 'fore them others even started." A shot, then another, came from the creek as the Comanche were still engaged with the carnage.

The boiling mass of wooly beasts continued to pass, storming over the small creek and leaving a wide mud hole for the others to wade through, but the tide never ebbed until after Cora and Rachel had left to return to the camp. Feather had said the downed animals would be tended to by the villagers, freeing them to return. It was almost like swimming against the tide when Cora and Rachel started back to the camp. The women and children were already starting to the valley for the work of skinning and butchering the buffalo. Although the men would help, it was mostly considered women's work, and it would be all day and much of the next before the butchering was done. They would not leave the kill site until every animal was stripped of every usable part, bladders to be used as water carriers, intestines for prepared cuts to be smoked, livers, hearts, sinews, and bones for marrow.

As Cora and Rachel rode up to their canvas lean-to, constructed from the bonnet of their wagon, Feather was tending to Reuben and looked up as the women dismounted. She looked to Reuben and back to the women, "He is good."

Reuben leaned around his attentive nurse and said, "Hi Ma, Rachel. You two do alright?"

"Yeah, we only dropped three apiece. Didn't wanna take too many."

Feather turned to look at Cora, wide-eyed, and asked, "You shot three buffalo?"

"Ummhumm, so'd Rachel."

Feather let a slow smile cross her face as she stood, "Then we should go. The others . . . uh, well, it is best if we go before they return."

Cora smiled and understood, "We'll get the mules loaded an' ready. Reuben's horse seems to be alright, so mebbe we can put the travois on him. He's purty gentle, and that way you won't have to drag him behind your'n." Feather nodded her head and went to retrieve her mount and packs.

Feather led the way with Cora and Rachel each leading

two pack-mules and Rachel bringing up the rear. Cora turned around in her saddle to check on her daughter and saw her staring into the distance, glassy eyed. She knew the girl was hopeful of seeing the wagons or maybe a certain boy returning on the trail, but Cora wasn't hopeful of ever seeing anyone from the wagons again.

Rachel was looking to the valley below, but she was deep in thought and those thoughts were about the conversations she and Michael had shared. The few times they had to themselves, their talks were always about the future and being together. Although Rachel was only fourteen and Michael a year older, they thought they were old enough to know their own minds and hearts, and eagerly talked about marriage and a home together. Rachel sighed heavily, not wanting to let go of those dreams, wondering how they could ever find one another again.

THE SUN WAS NESTLED between two distant peaks of the San Juan mountains and cast its last colors across the cloud littered sky, each cottony puff catching a different hue of the golds, oranges, and reds of the disappearing day. The long bands of color faded into the darkening blue overhead and seemed to point to the small caravan following the treeline trail that overlooked the waves of the sand dunes. Feather stopped and turned aboard her mount to look to the sunset. She didn't speak, and the other women, who had been twisting and swiveling to take in the sight, also stopped and stared in silence at the panoramic beauty. A slight edge of gold marked the descending orb that cast differing shadows on the mountains before them, turning each layer of mountains into a darkening jagged edged silhouette. When the sun's last bright arch disappeared, Feather looked to the others, "We are almost there. It's just there, in those trees."

And she turned toward the trees and clucked her horse forward.

As they broke into the clearing, Cora saw a broad-shouldered man set his rifle against the porch rail as a redheaded woman took the steps two at a time, smiling broadly and shouting, "Feather! Oh, it's so good to see you." By the time she reached the shaman's horse, Feather was already on the ground, arms spread wide, to accept the greeting of the woman. Cora watched the smiling man slowly descend the steps and start toward the visitors. When the redhead released Feather, the shaman was given a bear hug by the man.

It was only after the greetings were done, when the residents turned to the visitors and asked Feather, "So, what have you brought us this time?"

CHAPTER TWENTY-ONE
STORMS

THE GREY CANOPY OF A CLOUDY SKY HUNG LOW OVERHEAD AS Tate sat on the split log bench on the shoulder of the mountain that held his home. A break in the towering spruce before him gave a narrow window to the valley below and beyond. It was his custom to spend the early moments of the day communing with his Lord and enjoying the peaceful quiet of the morning. An early rising meadowlark sang his welcome to the man of the mountains and Tate let a smile cross his face as he listened.

"Good morning sweetheart," spoke Tate quietly without turning.

"You always know, no matter how quiet I am. How do you do that?" asked Maggie as she placed her hand on his shoulder to stand behind him. She bent to kiss him on his cheek and he placed his hand over hers.

He grinned broadly as he took her hand to guide her around the end of the bench to join him. He closed his Bible and sat it on the seat to his left and seated her on his right. He put his arm around her shoulder and drew her near, "I can always tell when you're near, and I know you can do the same with me. But, I learned a long time ago that if you pay attention, your senses will tell you of others nearby or of threatening danger. It's that feeling in the back of your neck when someone is behind you, or that gut sensation when you know someone is watching. That's why, whenever you see someone at a distance and you don't want them to know you're around, never stare at them. But, sometimes it's just paying attention. For example, those wagons down below . . ."

"Wagons? Where?" interrupted Maggie.

"Down there, about half-way between the creek in the bottom and the tree line. You can't see them from here, but they're there. They stopped there yesterday and they're the bunch that ran off and left our new visitors."

"When Feather told us about that, I couldn't hardly believe it! I mean, for the whole bunch of 'em to leave a woman and her kids behind, they need to be whipped!"

"Whoa, Maggie! I didn't mean to get that Irish temper ta' boilin'! But you're right, however, as you well know, you can't expect much from some of these pilgrims, especially when they're gold hungry. They prob'ly figgered these folks were done for and there wasn't enough o' them to take on the Comanche, even though all they were doin' was funnin' 'em." He chuckled at the memory of Feather laughing as she told how their warriors just yelled and kicked up dust to chase the wagons to get them away from the buffalo.

"Still, they could have at least made an effort," pouted Maggie.

They were both surprised when another voice chimed in, "They were running too fast!" said Feather as she walked up behind them, chuckling.

"Well, sometimes it takes more than the usual challenges to see the true measure of a man," surmised Tate, smiling.

"And that bunch down there is going to be measured again, I'm sure."

"What do you mean?" asked Maggie, her brow furrowing.

"Look at them clouds o'er there. I've been watchin' the beginnin' of a lightning show and that tells me we're gonna be gettin' some rain, maybe some hail. And those pilgrims down there are gonna get a lesson 'bout flash floods and adobe. And that's not even mentioning that bunch o' the Llaneros Jicarilla that have joined up with the Muache Ute. I think they're the bunch that hit Fort Pueblo last Christmas and there's a bunch o' young warriors that have banded together and I'm thinkin' they're up to no good. When I ran into that band here 'while back, there was both Apache and Ute up in that valley where Sean got his elk."

Both the women were quiet as they considered what Tate said, Feather especially because the combined bands of the Muache Ute and Llaneros Jicarilla Apache were enemies of the Comanche.

Maggie dropped her head as she thought about what would happen to the people of the wagons if they were attacked. Nine wagons with maybe a dozen men to fight off a band of eager young warriors with twice as many would not last long before the people of the wagons were annihilated. She shook her head at the thought, then lifted her face with a smile, "Well, I came out here to call you for breakfast! Are you ready?"

———

ALL THE MEMBERS of the wagon train had gathered near the wagon of George Garmin and the two leaders stood before the small crowd by the first light of the day. George began, "We've talked it over and agreed it would be best to stay here for a day to give the teams a good rest. There's grass by the creek, fresh water," the wagons had been circled up astraddle of the small creek, giving easy access to the fresh water, "and this bit of a basin we're in will give us enough protection from any Indians that might be roamin' the flats around." He waved his hands to take in the vast valley that lay before the towering mountains of the Sangre de Cristo range. Garmin's wife, Edna, and Michael stood behind him. Edna had the fingers of her right hand entangled in the shirtsleeve of her son, and her other hand through the crook of his arm. She pulled him close to her and Michael looked back at his mother. She saw the muscles in his cheek tighten as he gritted his teeth and his nostrils flared to show his anger. She knew he was remembering the arguments with his father and her mind went back to the scene beside their wagon.

"But pa! We gotta go back! Somethin's happened, I know it has, and they prob'ly need our help!"

"They're dead, that's what's happened! And you're not going back to sacrifice yourself for no good cause! Don't you know what those Injuns'll do to you? Look at your ma, boy! Do you think she wants to see your bloody body with arrows in it and your scalp taken?!"

"I don't plan to be taken! But they need our help! We can't just leave 'em! I'll go by myself if I have to!" shouted the frustrated Michael, stomping his feet and shaking his fist at his father.

George Garmin scowled at his son, lowered his voice to a menacing tone, "Don't you ever speak to me like that again. If I have to chain you to the wheel of this wagon, I will. You are not going anywhere! Do you hear me, boy?"

Michael had never seen his father this determined and angry and he stepped back out of reach of the man, fearful he would be struck down. He looked over to his mother and she dropped her eyes to the ground. Michael breathed heavily, calming down and said, "I hear you."

Now he stood beside his mother, listening to his father instruct the other families of the wagon train. He slowly shook his head, almost imperceptibly, and stared at the ground as his father continued.

"'Sides that, I think we could all use a day o' rest and time to repair the wagons after that run we took 'em on."

Ethel Northrup waved her hand in the air for attention and asked, "Find out anything 'bout the Ritter's?"

"No, no, from what we know them Comanche or what'ever kind o' Injuns they were, done got 'em. It's too bad, they was good people. Mebbe if she'd a had a man, he would'a been able to handle that wagon an' they might'a made it, but . . . " explained Harold Greene, exasperated at his inability to explain himself. He had been against taking a wagon with only a woman, but he had been overruled. His smug attitude showed as he explained to the others. "We'll post a watch at all times, don't wanna get caught again, so ever' man'll take his turn at watch. With a good day of rest and repair, tomorrow will be a good day for travelin'," he pointed to the rising clouds to the west, "an' we might get a little rain to settle the dust."

The somber crowd dispersed to their fires to start the cooking for the first meal of the day, most already had coffee on the fire and several wagons doubled up at the fire to save on gathering the scarce firewood or buffalo chips. The Northrup's and the Honeycutt's were sharing a fire, and the two men and two Honeycutt brothers were seated on a bench and boxes sipping their coffee when Ethel Northrup asked, "Did that Greene fella just guess at what happened to the Ritter's or did somebody go back and check on 'em?" She directed her question to all the men and looked from one to another for an answer.

"I don't think they had anybody go back an' check on 'em. I know Reuben took off up thataway, but ain't nobody seen him since either," answered Matthew Honeycutt, the older of the two brothers. "Far's I know, none o' the other scouts went back, an' Greene an' them was busy with their own wagons, so no, nobody really checked on 'em."

"Yeah, but Matthew, you saw all them Injuns, what good would it have done for anybody to go check? We'd just been killed too!" said his brother, Luke.

Fred Honeycutt and Sidney Northrup nodded their heads in agreement and Fred added, "The rest of us were more concerned about getting our own families outta there. If we'da tried to turn a wagon around, we'da lost everything." It was the rationale of the cowardly and selfish, those that always found a way to justify their choices and decisions afterwards. The world has always been full of people that rode on the coattails of the brave and the enterprising that made decisions in the instant of need, and the new west of the territories was no different. Many of the pilgrims that set out to pioneer the new lands would turn back because of hardships, and others would simply give up because they were unprepared, physically and mentally, to face up to the challenges of a new world. It was the few individuals that always found a way to do right and were willing to make the sacrifice necessary, no matter the circumstances, that would build a strong and free nation.

Ethel Northrup looked from man to man, each one dropping his gaze at her stare, shook her head and turned back to the fire. She lifted the lid on the dutch oven, looked at the biscuits, replaced the lid and shoveled more coals on top. She stood and went to the tailgate of the wagon where Hazel Honeycutt was slicing the pork belly into the cast iron skillet and Hazel spoke quietly, "It don't do no good to talk to 'em 'bout such things. They think they know more'n us women and we wouldn't understand. I just hope next time it ain't one of us that gets left behind."

"Hummph, they're so set on gettin' to the gold field, if we're late gettin' supper, they'd be tempted to leave us behind. 'Course, once they had to eat their own cookin' they'd be comin' back for us!" answered Ethel.

Hazel laughed, "Ya got that right, for sure an' certain!"

———

TATE HAD Reuben's arm around his shoulder and Tate had his around the young man's waist as the two hobbled together to the porch steps. The Ritter's had taken up residence in the wall tent of the trader, Barclay, as suggested by Tate, believing the trader would not be back for several days yet. Tate looked at the young man and said, "Let me get you up the stairs," and reached down to pick up the splinted leg with the other and lifted Reuben off his feet effortlessly. Reuben just looked at Tate, surprised, as he carried him up the steps and lowered his legs to the plank floor and said, "Let me help you to the bench there." Once Reuben was settled, Tate sat in his chair beside Maggie's rocker and leaned back to look at the youngsters playing in the clearing.

The air had turned cool and the wind was picking up, warning of the coming storm. Tate looked to the sky above the treeline, saw the grey bottomed clouds with fingers of lightning stretching to the ground and said, "It'll be here right quick," and lifted his voice to be heard by the laughing youngsters. Rachel was playing with Sean, Sadie, and Lobo, as Tate called, "Better get up here 'fore the storm hits, you're gonna get mighty wet!"

Reuben watched the three cavorting with the wolf and said, "I just can't get over you and that wolf! I never thought I'd see such a thing, and he's so big!"

"Yeah, but he's one o' the family. I can't even begin to tell you of the times he's saved our bacon. Did Sean tell you we also had a playmate for Lobo for a while?"

"A playmate? No, he didn't say anything about it. What was it, a bear?"

Tate looked at Reuben, laughed and said, "Yup."

"No! You didn't! Surely not, not a bear? I was just funnin'."

"We called him Buster. That's how Sean got his Indian name, Bear Chaser. He was named by the chief of the Caputa Ute, a friend of ours, Two Eagles."

Reuben looked at the man with wonder, thinking what he said was true, but still finding it hard to believe. He looked around at the cabin, the woods, the mountains, the family, and took a deep breath, as he began to think how this kind of life was very appealing to him. He never had any interest in California, except for the adventure of traveling and getting away from Missouri, but to consider a way of life, this mountain living seemed to be drawing him and he wasn't resisting.

Rachel and Sadie made it up the steps, but Sean was still wrestling with Lobo when the rain came. The sudden downpour was a cloudburst familiar to the mountains, and the two were soaked by the time they cleared the steps and made the landing of the porch. And as is true with all canines, Lobo shook the water from his fur, getting everyone wet and making them duck away from the unwanted shower. At their outburst, Maggie came to the door to see what the commotion was all about and stepped out to see the rain. Feather and Cora followed Maggie, and everyone stood looking as the big drops came at an angle and were already pooling in the clearing and beginning the run downhill.

"This is gonna be quite a gully washer!" said Tate, watching the torrent.

Suddenly Lobo came to his feet and looked to the edge of the clearing and a shout came, "Hey! Turn it off!" as the sodden figure of a man on horseback came into the clearing, trailed by four heavy laden mules.

Tate reached inside the doorway for his jacket and hat, and started down the stairs, buttoning his jacket and said, "Wondered when you'd get back. You could'a waited till it quit rainin'!"

"You know there ain't no place back yonder to wait out no rainstorm! This hyar's the onliest place thar is, and from all them on the po'ch, looks like you got a house-full!"

"Always room for one more, but in this case, not much room."

The two friends busied themselves derigging the animals and putting the packs in the back corners of the lean-to. It was a considerable stack of goods, but there was still ample room for sheltering the animals. Although Tate never thought of having this many animals in his corrals at one time, he had prepared a sizable lean-to shelter and the horses and mules were already crowding under cover from the deluge.

"Judging from your rig, it 'pears you've purty well decided on leavin' this country," observed Tate, stashing the gear out of the rain.

"Wal, mebbe. I'm kinda leanin' thataway, but it's mighty perplexin' as I think on it. Been in this hyar country a long time. Come out when I weren't no more'n a pup. Don't know no different, but I think I'm feelin' the wanderlust a mite."

"I know what you mean. I've been up an' down these mountains from the Missouri to the Rio Grande, and I still ain't seem 'em all. Ever onct in a while, I find myself lookin' yonder," nodding his head to the west, "an' wonderin' what's on the other side."

The two friends fell quiet as they finished stowing the gear and walked through the downpour, enjoying the cold rain, back to the cabin.

CHAPTER TWENTY-TWO
FLOOD

THE DELUGE CAUGHT THEM BY SURPRISE AND THEY JUMPED into the wagons, under the wagons, anywhere to get out of the downpour. Those that didn't make it to some cover, soon regretted their choice and climbed up to be protected under the canvas bonnets and in the company of others. The heavy battering on the canvas sounded more like hail, but the big drops of rain fell without any sign of letting up and muffled the conversation within. The mules milled about, drawing close to one another, trying to turn their tails to the force of the storm, but with the whirling winds, they gave up, dropped their heads and lowered their long ears to try to escape the worst of the tempest.

There was little let-up to the gale and the wagons rocked with the wind as well as the movements within. Muffled shouts that were attempts at conversation soon gave way to silence as each one tried to find some semblance of comfort to wait out the weather and maybe get some sleep in the meantime. Jesse Whitman and Conrad Eichman had been on guard but stayed at their post only moments before heading to the wagons, both believing there was no danger of attack from anyone or anything in this storm.

The storm had shown itself to be more than a simple cloudburst and after two hours of continual downpour, another sound brought Liam O'Toole wide awake as he sat up to listen. It sounded like the roar of far-away thunder. His eyes grew wide when he realized it wasn't just a moment of sound, but an ongoing rumble that was increasing and growing in intensity. The O'Toole wagon was next to the creek on the mountain side of the circle, and across the small stream was the Greene's wagon. Harold Greene was also attentive to the roar, not understanding but wondering, as he went to the back of the wagon to part the canvas to look out. The canvas popped and snapped in the wind as he pushed the flaps aside to see into the darkness of midday in the heavy deluge. He could see the light shining through the canvas in the wagon behind his, just across the creek that was running higher than before. The face of Liam O'Toole peered from the canvas, and his hair was sopped and over his eyes in an instant, he pushed it aside, saw Greene, and hollered, "What is it!?"

Greene could barely make out the words, but answered, "I don't know! Do you see anything?" and both men looked toward the mountains, but the rain was too heavy, and they could see but a few feet. The roar seemed to be increasing and coming from the mountains and Greene said, "Must be on the mountains, maybe a rockslide!"

"Yeah! Could be!" answered O'Toole as he ducked back inside the wagon.

Greene looked toward the mountains again and was troubled because the roar was continuing and increasing. He thought, *That ain't no rockslide, it's comin' toward us! Oh, no!*

The wall of water hit the wagons, tumbling the first two over on their sides and pushed past them to the others on the opposite side of the circle. The muddy tide smashed against two more wagons, pushing them aside as if they were boats on a dock. Because those wagons had parked farther from the stream bed, they were not dumped over, but shook and were pushed aside like toys. The roar of the floodwaters was deafening, and the screams of the O'Toole's and Greene's went unheard in the melee. Mules pushed against the wagons away from the stream, and the wagons rocked like a cradle in the hand of a drunken mother. George Garmin was knocked to the side of his wagon with such force, his weight split the wooden bow and his hand at the edge of the wagon box was all that kept him from ripping through the canvas. He looked to his wife and son, "Are you alright?" he hollered, and saw the nodding heads of both.

Garmin stepped to the tailgate and pushed aside the canvas. The storm had not abated, and he could only see the wagon behind theirs and the faint image of the wagon beyond. He craned around to look at the mules, that were shaking and prancing nervously, but their milling around was not that unusual for the high-spirited animals. He ducked back inside and said, "I can't see anything. We'll have to wait till this storm lets up and then check on everyone." He heard the continuing roar, but thought it was just the wind and the storm and settled back into the wagon with his family. He grabbed the big quilt that he used before and wrapped back up to snuggle down and sleep.

Several of the others let their curiosity get the better of them and they too ventured a peek out of their canvas bonnets. But each was hampered in his visual search and unknowingly copied the actions of one of the captains, George Garmin, and settled back into their wagons to wait out the storm.

When the wall of water hit the Greene wagon, it tumbled over to its side. The unstoppable force picked up the wagon and dropped it wheels up and ripped at the canvas. Harold and Gertrude were side by side when the water hit and held tightly to one another as the wagon tumbled in the water. When the last surge dumped it upside down, the couple were trapped under the weight of two big trunks and a chifforobe, fought for breath and clung to one another in their last moment. The younger Greene, sixteen-year-old Hank, was using the wagon seat for his perch and when the water hit, he was thrown to the side, but his feet were entangled in the canvas. He fought, kicked, and with a deep breath, grabbed his knife from the scabbard at his waist and hacked away at the canvas and was finally freed. He fought through the muddy mass to get air, and the racing current carried him away.

The O'Toole's, Kathleen and her thirteen-year-old daughter, Margaret, had huddled together for warmth when Liam had opened the canvas for a look-see. When the torrent of water hit their wagon, it was banged to its side, and the women were thrown into the bows and canvas. Kathleen was knocked unconscious and Margaret was beneath her, entangled in the canvas and the broken bows. She fought and kicked, underwater all the time, and pushed at her mother's body, fighting for air and pushed away, but was suddenly struck in the head by a heavy boot and knocked unconscious. She fell back alongside her mother and the last bubbles of air slipped from her lips, watched by open eyes.

Liam fought to get free of the broken wagon box and all the barrels and trunks it held. He was in a panic and pushed blindly, thrashing at the water when he suddenly felt canvas. He thought he was at the top of the wagon and the surface of the water, he kicked with his heavy miner's boots, felt something give and stepped on whatever it was and found air. He splashed away from the wagon, but a tree trunk of an uprooted pine stretched out its long branches and drug him under as it rolled with the current of the flood.

———

As the storm weakened, the crowd in the narrow confines of the cabin joined the men on the porch. Lex jumped out of Maggie's rocker and motioned for her to take her seat, and he stepped to the rail to lift one haunch and sit. Feather and Cora joined Reuben on the long bench below the window and Rachel and the youngsters seated themselves beside Lobo on the planked floor. "So, have you men got everything all figured out with your talking and conspiring out here on the porch?" asked Maggie, grinning at Tate.

"Didn't need to, already knew the answers to ever'thing!" declared Tate seriously.

All the women laughed at his response and Cora said, "Ummhumm, you're just like all the rest. Think ya' know ever'thing!"

"What? You mean I don't? Now, how 'bout you enlightenin' me with all your worldly knowledge and I'll tell you if there's something I don't already know!"

"Wal, Tate, I thot'chu knew ever'thing. Ya' know a darn sight more'n I do, anyways!" chimed in Lex.

"He told me he knew everything," answered Reuben, shaking his head in agreement with Lex.

"My pa knows ever'thing, don't he Sadie Marie?" insisted Sean.

"Ummhumm, he knows!" agreed Sadie.

"Now, you gonna argue with your own children?" asked Tate, grinning.

"Oh you, that's one thing you do know, is how to weasel out of just about any corner!" answered Maggie, smiling.

"So, how do you think those wagons did in this storm?" asked Cora.

Tate looked at her, somewhat surprised, "I didn't think you'd be too worried about them, not after what they done."

"Wal, I wouldn't give two cents for the whole bunch of 'em, but that don't mean I oughta be like 'em, do it?" asked the woman.

"You're right about that. Where they were camped, they coulda been hit by a flash flood comin' off these mountains, but even if they did, there's not much we can do for 'em now. They'll just have to pick up the pieces and keep goin'," answered Tate. "But I s'pose we could check on 'em in the mornin', just to see if they need any help." His remarks came from a curiosity of the woman's concern and compassion. He had every intention of providing all the help possible, as was his nature, but he didn't know Cora well enough to understand what might be her true sentiments.

"That'd be good," answered Cora, "Ya' don't suppose you could do it without them knowin' I was here, could'ja?"

"Sure, me'n Lex could go down an' check on 'em. They don't need to know you're here."

Lex piped up and asked, "Say, ma'am, Tate tells me you're a gunsmith, that right?"

"Ummhumm, grew up in my pa's shop and learned from him. He was the best, 'cordin' to all the folks round 'bout where we lived. Been doin' it my own self since 'fore these youngun's was borned," replied Cora, looking at the trader somewhat suspiciously.

"Wal, I tooken in some rifles an' such in trade at muh tradin' post. Some of 'em could use a mite a work, if'n you was interested. Course, I'd pay ya fer whatcha do."

"Ya, don't say. I guess I could take a look at what'cha got." The trader and the gunsmith were eyeballing one another as they talked.

Tate and Maggie watched the conversation and were both thinking the two were thinking about more than fixing trade rifles. Maggie looked at Feather and knew she recognized the signs of romantic interest as well. The three smiled conspiratorially and chuckled to themselves. At the pause in their conversation, Tate said, "There's a workbench in the tack shed yonder. You could use that if you like, Cora."

"What?" she asked and looked to the smiling Tate and answered, "Oh, uh, yeah, that'd be good."

Tate stood and looked around, "Well, fellas, looks like we got the tent and the women and kids have the cabin. So, how 'bout we turn in and get us a early start to check on the wagons, what say?"

"Suits me! How's 'bout I help you with the younker there an' get him off'n the porch so we can get to them bedrolls, assumin' they still high'n dry!" answered Lex.

CHAPTER TWENTY-THREE
TROUBLE

ONCE THE RAIN BEGAN TO LET UP, THE DWINDLING LIGHT OF day revealed the desolation among the wagons. Garmin was the first to stick his head out of the canvas to look around. The sight of overturned wagons startled a gasp from the man and he jumped from his wagon to look at the rest of the circle. The half-buried wagon with wheels up, he recognized as the Greene's because of its placement in the circle. Mud had swept up and over the wagon box, leaving silt, mud and branches of uprooted trees making the wheels partially buried in the debris. Across the creek, now running full with muddy flood water, the end of the O'Toole wagon stuck up from the edge of the water like a shipwreck, canvas ripped and strung out along the creek bank like a flag of desperation.

Garmin's first step slipped out from under him and he landed on his rump in the slick adobe mud. He twisted around and grabbed at the wagon wheel to pull himself erect and wiped his hands on the wagon box before starting for the Greene wagon. Fred Honeycutt and Sidney Northrup were climbing out of their wagons, "Be careful there, this mud's mighty slick!" warned Garmin.

"Is that the Greene wagon," asked Northrup, stepping down from his tailgate.

"'Peers to be," answered Garmin.

The three men stopped before the wagon, mostly buried in the mud, and Northrup asked, "Ya don't s'pose there's anybody under there, do ya?"

"If they ain't there, they musta been washed down the creek!" answered Honeycutt. "We oughta get some shovels and have a look see anyway, don'tcha think?"

"Yup," responded Garmin, then lifted his eyes to the wagons across the creek. "We'll need to get somebody o'er there to check on that wagon." He spotted Lee Cutler sticking his head out of his wagon's bonnet and hollered, "Hey Lee, can you check on that wagon? See if there's anybody in there?" Cutler lifted his hand in a wave and pushed his way through the canvas to step down from the box.

The mud was soft, and the digging was easy. Once the tailgate was clear, Garmin and Honeycutt lifted, while Northrup bellied down to look inside. The mud had swirled around and there was little space left inside, trunks, boxes hindered the search, but Northrup called out, "Got two bodies here, looks like Greene and his woman!" Northrup backed out of the wagon and the men dropped the tailgate. "It'll be easier to dig around the wagon and flip it back over. We ain't gonna get 'em outta there otherwise."

"Mebbe we oughta just put up a cross with their names on it an' leave 'em where they be!" suggested Honeycutt. The other men looked at him, surprised, "Wal, if it ain't one thing it's another, an' ever'day we waste, somebody else is gettin' the gold!" he declared disgustedly. He was the first to voice what the others had been thinking. But to hear it said, Garmin and Northrup felt the bile rise in their throats.

"Hey!" came the shout from across the creek. Lee Cutler cupped his hands to his mouth and said, "Looks like the whole family's under there! All three of 'em!"

Honeycutt tried to stomp his foot in disgust, but it slipped out from under him and he slid down the slight embankment to the water. He rolled over and clawed at the thick adobe mud to escape from the floodwaters. Northrup dropped to a knee and extended his hand, with his other held by Garmin, and the teamwork brought Honeycutt to safety. When he struggled to his feet, he was covered with the slimy mud head to toe. He spat mud, tried to wipe his face with muddy hands, and fussed and fumed. "Let's leave all this till mornin', let this mud dry out some. Otherwise, we'll all look like we done been buried and crawled outta the grave!" He stomped off to his wagon without waiting for an answer. It was evident by his demeanor and refusal to describe what he had seen that he found no sign of life. The word passed from wagon to wagon and the entire train turned in for the night without supper but with a belly full of emotions.

TATE AND LEX BARCLAY sat easy in their saddles just inside the treeline and looked to the wagons by the early morning light. They could see the activity around wagons that sat on both sides of the creek. The stream had subsided to its usual low flow and clear water, making it easy for the people to get across using the rock they had placed mid-stream. It was obvious they were digging graves and Tate shook his head as Lex said, "There just ain't no end to how dumb some o' these pilgrims show themselves to be. Ain't nobody in their right mind makes camp astraddle a stream. Pilgrims!" he spat in disgust. His anger at the stupidity of the settlers, like so many others, that had resulted in unnecessary deaths. He had known too many times when lives could have been saved if those in the decision-making positions would just set aside their pride and use some common sense. But he knew the greed for gold blinded many to the need for caution.

They moved out of the trees, picking their route across the grassy stretches, knowing the footing in the adobe would still be slick and a horse could easily have a hoof slide and be upended in an instant. They heard one of the people by the wagons call out, "Riders!" The alarm making everyone stop and grab for their rifles and take cover.

Tate held up one hand and called out, "We're friendly, just checkin' to see if everyone's alright!"

"Come ahead on if'n you're friendly, keep your hands empty!" declared George Garmin.

As they drew near, Tate spoke, "Howdy folks. I'm Tate, and this here's Lex. Looks like you folks had a little difficulty. Them flash-floods off the mountains can sure do some damage. Looks like you're diggin' some graves, lose somebody didja?"

"Not that its any your concern, but yeah, we had some folks get caught when their wagon went down. What are you white men doin' in these parts?"

Tate was quick to pick up on the attitude of the speaker and looked around at the others. They were a ragged looking bunch, but that was partly because of the storm, but the set of their jaws, their eyes cut to slits, the men still holding their rifles at the ready, told Tate all he needed to know. These people were suspicious of everyone and didn't want any interference with their already determined plans. Tate looked to Lex and said, "Well, partner, looks like we done wore out our welcome. What say we just go away and leave these folks alone?"

"Suits me," answered Barclay as he looked over the bunch

of pilgrims, disgust showing in his tone. Both men reined their mounts around and without another word, started back to the trees.

————

GARMIN TURNED BACK to look at the others, some shaking their heads as they turned away from their leader. "Well, we didn't know nuthin' 'bout 'em, an' we done wasted 'nuff time as it is. Let's get these folks buried and get on our way. We can't get outta this mudhole soon 'nuff for me!" The others didn't respond, but those digging and preparing bodies returned to their tasks without comment.

The stream that had dealt the death blow was known as Sand Creek. Coming from high in the mountains, it marked the northern edge of the sand dunes and trailed off to the west to be swallowed by the dry sandy valley. The co-captains of the wagon train knew the mules could make it no further when they chose to camp along the first stream they came to after their runaway flight from the Comanche. They felt they would be well protected with the dunes to the south, the mountains to their east, and a bit of a rise or swell to the land just north and west of them. It was a shallow basin that was chosen for their campsite that now became a grave site instead. As they were busy with the graves and stripping the wagons of the deceased, they failed to post a sentry, but they felt they would be leaving soon and were more concerned about their preparations. And as they had been so often reminded, they had lost enough time and needed to get underway before all the best gold claims were taken, they still had a long way to go to the goldfields of California.

TWO MEN WERE BELLY DOWN on a sand dune, looking over the

sharp-edged crest, watching the activity of the wagons. One had a quiver full of arrows across his back, the beaded pattern matching that of his moccasins. His buckskin leggings and breechcloth were almost the same color as the sand. Two braids of raven black hung by his shoulders, each with a notched feather at the base. The other man also had buckskin leggings and a breechcloth, but his hair hung loose, held in place by a woven cloth headband. His waist held a leather belt adorned with a scabbard that held a skinning knife and a metal bladed tomahawk was tucked at his side. When the man with the headband turned to the side, long porcupine quills protruded from both sides of his nose which told of his name, Quills-in-Nose, and he motioned to the other for them to leave. Both men shinnied back away from the crest, stood and used their heels to slow their descent down the slope to their horses. They swung aboard and turned away from the dunes and rode toward the south at a gallop and out of sight of the wagons.

TATE AND LEX RODE into the trees and were ascending the trail when it broke out into a small clearing atop a slight shoulder. Tate turned to look back toward the wagons and movement caught his eye. He said, "Lex, look!" and pointed to two horsemen riding at a gallop away from the wagons. "Those are Indians!"

"Yeah, they musta been spyin' on them wagons. You know what that means, don'tcha?"

"I'm afraid so, but those people aren't about to listen to anything we have to say."

"Prob'ly not. How 'bout we go talk to Cora 'bout 'em, she might know some way of getting' through to them fools!"

"The one that did the talkin', big guy, jowls, thin hair?" asked Cora.

"Yeah, that sounds like him. Sounded like a purty ornery cuss, didn't wanna have anything to do with us," answered Tate.

"Was there a thinner man, 'bout half a head taller, ruddy complexion and beady eyes?"

"Nope, didn't see anybody like him."

"Well the one you talked to sounds like Garmin, he's one o' the cap'ns. The other'n was the one I didn't get along with, thought there shouldn't be no woman alone on the train, his name was Greene."

"Well, they was diggin' five graves, an' three o' them crosses had the name Greene on 'em," said Lex.

"Five graves, huh, that's too bad," said Cora, softly. "So's, there any place where you think them Injuns might hit 'em that we can beat 'em to?"

"Uh, yeah, come to think of it. If they get outta that mud-hole by the creek, and they should, then from there on the way they're going, it's purty sandy and grassy, and they could prob'ly make it. It's about four or five miles to Deadman Creek, that's the next creek where there'll be any water. It's a purty good stream, got willows'n cottonwood, some alder. Maggie gets some o' the Indian potatoes an' such along there. We could get there by takin' a trail through the trees an' find us a spot to wait fer 'em. If the injuns hit 'em, they'll prob'ly come from the alkali flats where there's some rocks an' such to give 'em cover."

Cora looked at Tate and asked, "Alright if'n me an' Rachel come along? We both got Sharps and can hit what we aim at."

Tate looked at the woman, then to Rachel, and to Lex, "I'd 'preciate it if Rachel'd stay here with Maggie. She's pretty good with her Hawken, so's Sean. But, if for some reason them bucs decide to come through the trees, it'd be better to have a little more firepower here."

Rachel smiled and nodded to her mother, "I'd like that, Ma."

Tate stood, as did Lex, and said, "Then let's get to it!"

THEY MOVED AT A CANTER, Lobo leading the way as they cut through the black timber following the game trail that stayed well inside the treeline. The trail was well-used as it worked its way up the valley, low enough on the mountains to avoid the deeper ravines and ridges, but high enough to stay in the timber. A familiar trail to Tate, having been used for many of his hunting excursions into the upper end of the valley. The last time he traveled it was with his family to make their spring visit to the hot springs. The occasional thin spots in the trees afforded them a momentary glimpse into the valley and he knew they were well ahead of the wagons.

When the trail dropped into the shallow ravine of Deadman Creek, they crossed over and turned downstream, using the greenery to shield them from view of the wagons or the Indians. Tate dropped down to the stream where a thick bunch of cottonwood saplings would provide protection for the horses. They dismounted and walked below the bank and farther downstream toward an obvious crossing that would draw the attention of the wagons.

"Lex, you get you a good spot upstream here, an' me'n Cora'll go below the crossing. I'm thinkin' the attack'll come from that direction," he pointed to the southwest toward the alkali covered draw in the low of the valley, "and they'll need more help on this side. Cora said they usually have a couple scouts ahead o' train, so try to keep from bein' seen by 'em. Don't want 'em to give us away if any Indians are scoutin' 'em."

Lex nodded in understanding and said, "You two keep yore heads down too, unnerstand?"

"I do, an' I will," answered Cora.

"Yup," replied Tate as he pointed Cora to the thicker brush to take up her spot.

GARMIN DIDN'T BOTHER TALKING to any of the others about getting a replacement for the co-captain. He wasn't concerned about having to share the duty with anyone, it had been as much a bother as anything to have to always consult with Greene about everything. It didn't take long to realize the two men disagreed about just about everything, and now that he was in charge, he rose to the task. He even made Jesse Whitman cut the Scripture reading short as he stood over the new graves, saying they were in Indian country and they needed to be moving. And they were soon on their way, with the Honeycutt brothers sent ahead to scout, and hoped to make at least fifteen miles today.

But with the late start, their struggles to get free of the adobe that seemed to cling to the wheels and the mules' hooves, it was approaching midday when the greenery ahead indicated a stream. Matthew Honeycutt had ridden back and told Garmin in the lead wagon that there was a pretty good spot across the stream to stop for their nooning. Garmin nodded and said, "Pass the word, we'll stop on the other side. But it'll be a short stop, we ain't come far enough to spend much time here!" he demanded as he slapped reins to his mules. After moving away from the adobe mud near the last stream, the flats below the mountains had more grass and sand, and the going was a lot easier for the mules. But they needed water, and a chance to graze since the last camp had been overrun by mud.

Luke Honeycutt had dismounted at the stream and bellied down to get a drink when a voice came from the brush, "Don't move!"

He started to get up, but again the voice came, "I said, don't move! Now just keep on drinkin' like nothin's happenin' and listen real close. Understand? Nod your head if you do!"

The young man, still on his belly, hands at his sides and elbows sticking up in the air, nodded his head.

"I'm the fella that came into your camp this mornin', and we're friendly. But you got some folks followin' you that ain't so friendly. There's some Apache and Ute, young bucs lookin' for scalps an' guns, and they're workin' they way up behind your wagons and gettin' ready to attack."

The boy started to jump but was stopped, "Don't move!"

Tate was talking low and continued, "Now, we're ready to cut down on 'em from here. But, when them Indians attack, and we start shootin', I'm afraid your people'll think we're Indians too. So, you need to slowly get up," and he waited a moment for the young man to move, "and get back on your horse just like nothing's happenin', cuz there might be a scout fer them Indians a watchin' you. You can start walkin' your horse back toward the wagons, and when the attack comes, you order the lead wagons to keep comin', tell 'em we're here to help 'em. Understand?"

"Yessir, I understand. But shouldn't I warn the wagons?"

"You won't get there in time to warn 'em, them Apache are gettin' ready to attack now."

Luke mounted up and swung his horse around, trying not to look anywhere but back to the wagons and he started walking back toward them. He was less than a hundred yards from the wagons, when the brush beside the trail came alive as Indians rose to let arrows fly and those with rifles fired the first volley. Mounted warriors came from behind the rocky ridges beside the alkali bottoms and the wagons surged as men once again put the whips to the mules, their first thought to try to outrun the attackers.

Luke kicked his horse to a gallop and as he neared Garmin's wagon, he hollered, "Go to the crossing! There's friends there! Keep goin'!" Garmin looked at the young man but slapped the mules and stood to throw rocks at the lead mules as he screamed at them, "Heeeeyaahh mules! Move it!" An arrow whispered in front of his face and he ducked his head like a turtle and fell back on his seat, trying to make himself as small as possible as he shook out the reins at the mules.

The other wagons were chasing after the Garmin's and the screams and war cries of the attackers startled everyone, but the flight of arrows and the gunshots from the brush told them this was an even deadlier attack than the other had been. The Eichman wagon was just behind Garmin's but was gaining on the lead wagon. Conrad Eichman jerked on the reins of the lead mules and pointed them to the side of the Garmin wagon, not wanting to take any chances on not escaping. As they gained and came alongside, the lead mule of Garmin's took an arrow in the neck and stumbled, caught its balance and matched his mate stride for stride. Within a short distance, the mule stumbled again and fell, causing the mule behind to trip and fall as well. The crash of the wagon as it hit the downed team and tipped to its side, threw both George and Edna, screaming, over the backs of the other two mules. Michael was riding alongside on his horse, and reined around to help his parents. He slid to a stop and stepped down to pick his mother up. He lifted her up to the saddle and turned for his father but stopped when he saw his father's sightless eyes staring at the sky, his neck and body twisted at an awkward angle. The sudden thought of the last words shared with his father were in anger and he wanted to say, "I'm sorry," but he scream of a war cry nearby made Michael turn back to his mother and slap the horse on the rear for it to take off, but he kept a hand on the saddle horn and used the momentum of the horse as he dug in his heels and swung up behind his mother. He kicked at the horse's ribs and pointed it toward the crossing. As they fled, he wondered if the death of his father was some kind of retribution for his failure to help the Ritters, but he shook his head to rid himself of the thought and ran for the crossing.

IT WAS the Apache way to lay in wait for an attack. Tate had learned that these skilled warriors of the plains could hide where least expected and directly in front of an observer that searched the land before them. With dirt splattered on any exposed parts, and their ability to hold absolutely still, they were practically invisible even when someone looked directly at them. But Tate had picked out possible hiding places, whispered them to Cora, and was waiting for their move to attack. Within seconds of the first war cry as several rose from the small sage or greasewood to launch their arrows, the three Sharps rifles barked almost simultaneously as they sounded their message of death. But it was more than the accuracy of the shooters that turned the battle, but the rapidity of their reloading. With the shooters able to get off six to eight well placed shots in a minute, they sent a barrage of lead that met the attacking young bucs. The volley shocking those that had been certain of their success.

As their fellow warriors were blasted off their feet, some sent tumbling end over end, but more falling than remained, the others began searching for the dealers of death. One of their leaders, Cut Nose, had tried to direct the attack from below the rocky escarpment that separated the alkali flats from the trail, spotted the shooters along the bank of Deadman Creek. He screamed to two of his warriors, the same two that had spied on the wagons, Quills in Nose and Crazy Bear, and sent them to flank the shooters. They immediately ran to the lower end of Deadman Creek and started their stalk of the hidden riflemen.

In the midst of a battle, when many were falling, it seemed like hours or longer when it was only seconds or minutes. The wagons headed for the creek at a full run, bouncing and rattling as the drivers cracked whips and lines, screaming at the mules. The attackers, many on horseback, shouted their war cries and tried to overtake the wagons. Many of the warriors went to the uphill side, as shooting from horseback was most natural to have your quarry on your left. Whether using a bow and arrows, throwing a lance, or even shooting a rifle, it is easier to throw or shoot across your body to your target. But the crowded group of riders on the uphill side also became targets for Lex Barclay and the experienced mountain man. The men calmly aimed, fired, and reloaded their big Sharps, with almost every shot scoring a hit. Within the first moments of the attack, the scattered bodies of Indians and horses littered the slope that fell away from the mountains, and still the trader kept shooting. He was grinning all the time, almost enjoying the deadly game of death.

Many of the attackers had come from the sage and greasewood below the trail and others from the rocky slope near the alkali. Most of these were on foot and had lain in wait for their attack, but they had no protection from the shooters in the brush by the creek, and the big Sharps began to take their toll. The powerful .52 caliber rifles were deadly, even if the bullet hit a less than vulnerable spot, just the impact of such a large hunk of lead would tear away so much flesh that if a man was hit in the arm, it could easily tear it off his body. And the blast of the powder load was deafening and the sight of the powder smoke coming from the bushes was frightening.

Cora was not as calm as she hoped, and with each successive reload she saw her hands were shaking, but she struggled to keep at it. Tate was less than ten yards away and he shouted, "You alright?"

"Yeah, just a little scared is all," she replied as she dropped the lever on the sharps to lower the breech block and pluck out the remnants of the last shot. She was slipping another paper cartridge in when she looked in Tate's direction. He had his head down, looking at his rifle and reloading, but coming up beside him was an Apache Warrior, war club raised high to strike. She started to shout a warning, but the words wouldn't come, and she stuttered and waved her hand, but he wasn't looking. She reached for a rock to throw and get his attention, but she knew she couldn't warn him in time and she looked again, eyes wide and afraid.

Suddenly a streak of grey came from the brush and hit the warrior. Lobo's mouth was wide, and his long teeth clamped down on the throat of the Apache, the weight of the wolf carried them both to the ground. Even above the screams and sounds of battle, Cora heard the growls and snarls of the wolf. Beyond the Apache, another Indian saw the attack and the sight of his fellow warrior being taken down by a monstrous wolf sent him running away and screaming like a frightened child.

Tate saw Lobo doing his work but turned back to the attack before him and picked another shot, knocked a charging Indian from his horse, and dropped his rifle to reload. Cora watched in amazement, but knew she was needed, and she too picked her next shot.

TATE STOOD TO WATCH THE REMAINING ATTACKERS LEAVE. They shouted threats and war cries as they swung aboard their horses that had been tethered near the rocks and alkali. Tate guessed there were at least thirty attackers, but the ragtag bunch that left only numbered about a dozen. It had been a costly attack for the young bucs and hopefully they had learned a valuable lesson about the whites and wagon trains. In their flight, many of those on the wagons returned fire and many of those that handled the rifles were women and they had proven their mettle.

Tate walked to Cora's side and gave her a hand to her feet. She shook her head, showing her consternation with herself, held her shaking hand out to show her nervousness, "It's a wonder I was even able to reload, much less hit anything," she declared.

"You did fine. Couldn't have expected any better from an experienced mountain man."

Cora looked at him and let a smile of pride cross her face. She put her shoulders back and said, "Thanks Tate, that's high praise!" She looked around at the wagons that were now all on the north side of the creek and the people were climbing down to check their losses. "I'll go get the horses, you can check on that bunch."

Tate was greeted by Jesse Whitman and his wife, Cynthia, as he approached. They looked at the buckskin clad mountain man that had been shirked before and Jesse stepped forward, offering his hand, "Sir, we are very grateful to you and your friends. We never would have made it without your help. I'm afraid instead of dead Indians and horses out there," nodding across the creek, "there would be dead mules and all of us. You saved us sir, and we cannot thank you enough."

As he spoke some of the others came near, also extending hands to shake and express their thanks. As they took tally, they found Mildred Simpson had taken an arrow and fell from the wagon, under the wheels, and lay dead on the hillside among the Indians. Luke Honeycutt, the son of Fred and Hazel and one of the scouts, had taken an arrow in his back and was being tended to by his mother. As Tate looked them over, he knew it could have been much worse. Sidney Northrup approached and asked, "What do we do now? We lost both our captains, and we got a long way to go to California." His vexation showed as he looked to the others, none offering an answer.

Tate answered, "That's not up to me. I think you all were plumb foolish to come into this country with so few of you as it is, an' to do it without a guide that knows the country and the Indians, well . . . " he shook his head as he dropped his eyes to the ground.

"Would you guide us? You seem to know the country and the Indians," asked Northrup and several of the others nodded their heads in agreement with the suggestion.

"I'm not what you want for a guide, I ain't got much use for a bunch o' gold hungry pilgrims that forget their upbringing and are so willing to leave folks behind in their rush. No, I'm afraid I couldn't tolerate that way o' thinkin'. But I will tell you this, you need to get away from here, make a decent camp closer to the trees, an' there's plenty o' places straight ahead on this trail. But them Indians will be comin' back for their dead an' you don't wanna be here."

"Well, if we move out and camp like you said, will you at least think about it? Guidin' us, I mean," pleaded Northrup. It was hard for a man like him to ask help of anyone. Northrup had always been an independent type and asked help of no one, his father taught him that. He had owned a tavern in Westport and had been successful, but he also knew that business brought trouble with it and he never expected to get rich serving whiskey to freighters and pilgrims. When the thought of striking it rich in the goldfields took root in his mind, he knew it was probably his last opportunity for the big riches that was the subject of many dreams. He also knew if the gold didn't meet expectations, he could always put in another tavern and mine the miners for their gold.

Tate looked at the expectant faces and answered, "I'll consider it. But you need to think about something too. There's not enough of you to fight off another attack, and where you're going there will be plenty of Indians that want what you have, your horses, rifles, women, everything. There's Mouache Ute, some of which were with these Apache, Caputa Ute, Arapaho, Paiute, and more. And most of 'em would be glad to see your scalp hanging from their lances. So, here's what you need to think about. Go back to Bent's Fort and wait for another bunch o' pilgrims to join up with or go north to Fort Bridger on the Oregon Trail and join others. That's the only way I can see you folks livin' long enough to try your luck at pannin' gold. You think about that as you get on farther up yonder, bury your dead, and I'll come see you in the mornin'."

The entire group seemed to break out in smiles as they

nodded their heads and turned to their wagons. Tate walked back to the brush to join Lex and Cora and go back to the cabin. Cora and Lex were already mounted and as Tate swung aboard Shady, Cora said, "Look! There. That's a white man!" She pointed to a walking figure that was picking his way among the refuse and bodies of the battle ground.

Tate said, "Wait here!" and gigged his horse from the creek and toward the staggering man. His clothes were muddy, bloody, and torn. His hair was mussed, and his eyes glazed as he walked. When Tate rode up to him, he stopped and looked at the man on the horse, shaded his eyes and asked, "Pa?"

Tate stepped down and looked at the young man and said, "Were you with these wagons, son?"

The young man looked around, saw the broken wagon of the Garmin's, the bodies of several Indians and horses and mules. He looked back at Tate and said, "Yeah, but I don't see our wagon," he muttered as he stretched out a hand to Tate's horse to keep from falling.

"What's your name, boy?"

"Uh, uh, Hank, Hank Greene."

"Your pa's name Harold Greene?"

"Yeah, but I seen some graves back yonder, they had muh folks' names on 'em."

"I'm afraid so, son. You wanna come with us or do you wanna go to the wagons?" asked Tate, knowing the people of the wagons had left this young man just like they left Cora and her family.

"Who're you?"

"My name's Tate, Tate Saint. I live in these parts and I got a home back in the woods yonder. There's also some folks you know that are stayin' with me. You're welcome to come."

Hank stepped back to look at the man before him, then looked at the broken wagon and dead mules, then lifted his eyes to the white topped bonnets of the wagons beyond the creek and said, "Sure, I'll go with you. They left me."

Tate swung back aboard Shady, kicked his foot free of the stirrup and offered a hand to the worn-out young man and lifted him up to sit behind the cantle of his saddle. He rode back to the brush, nodded to Cora and Lex, and started back to the cabin.

MAGGIE STOOD with hands on hips as she watched the returning Indian fighters. Feather stood beside her, and Maggie said to Tate, "If you keep doin' this, you're gonna have to build on more rooms to this wilderness hotel!" She smiled at her returning husband and went down the steps to give him a proper welcome.

Feather leaned against the porch post as she grinned at her two friends, turned back to Rachel and said, "They are always that way."

Maggie pushed herself back from Tate and looked at his smiling face. "We heard a lotta shooting! It's good to see you don't have any holes in you."

Tate patted his body as if looking for wounds and said, "Well, no new ones at least!" and laughed with his wife. He turned to the young man standing beside him and said, "Maggie, this is Hank Greene. His folks were buried down yonder, they got caught in the flood. This young man was washed away and found his way back, but the wagons had left him. So, . . . "

Maggie turned her smiling face to the new addition and said, "Welcome Hank. I suppose you know . . . " and she was interrupted by Rachel who had come from the porch to see who was with them. "Hank? Hank! Oh, I thought when Tate said there were graves with markers that said, Greene, I thought you were gone!" She reached up to give him a hug which he gladly returned.

"Me? We thought all you had been killed by the Indians!"

Rachel laughed and said, "No, they were just funnin' with us! They weren't attacking! Come on, I want you to meet White Feather. She helped us."

Maggie and Tate watched the two friends walk back to the porch happily talking with one another. Rachel looked to Hank, "What about Michael, is he alright?"

"He was when I last saw him. But he an' his pa weren't gettin' along. I think Michael was mad about nobody goin' back to help you folks. He told me he was goin' by himself if he had to, but his pa lit into him sumpin' awful. I didn't get to talk to him after that."

"What about the flood, were they alrigh?"

"I dunno, they left me too."

Rachel looked at her friend, shook her head sadly and sat beside him on the porch.

MAGGIE TURNED TO TATE, "WHAT NOW?"

"I don't know," he shook his head and picked up the reins of Shady to take him to the corral as Maggie walked beside him. "That bunch o' folks," he shook his head again, "I don't think there's a lick o' common sense among 'em. They're so dead set on gettin' to the goldfields, and there ain't enough of 'em to make it. They asked me to guide 'em and I said I weren't interested, but still . . . "

Maggie looked at her man and knew this compassionate man whom she loved had a hard time saying no to anyone in need. That was one of the things she loved about him, but she feared for him as well. Their last few years together had been the best ever, better than she ever hoped she could have, but time changes things and now the frontier was so different than when they first came back to this cabin. With so many wagon trains bringing settlers out from the east, the many tribes of Indians trying to keep their lands and way of life, it was a constant conflict and an escalating one. They had talked about it before and had discussed moving back to the Wind River Mountains where Tate had lived with his first wife. They had agreed that if there was anything or anyone who would require his help, they would be in it together and she and the children would not be left behind. Even with their friendship with the many different bands of Indians, there were still those that had reckless young bucs or renegades that could make living in the mountains very dangerous.

"Well, how far would we have to go?" asked Maggie, emphasizing the 'we'.

Tate looked at his wife and chuckled, remembering their conversations and said, "I'm not sure. I told 'em to think about going back to Bent's Fort or up the Fort Bridger to hook up with another wagon train, but they're so set on gettin' to the goldfields, who knows what they'll decide."

"Well, I've got a big elk roast that's about ready, so, soon's you finish here, come on to supper. Maybe we can all talk about it together."

Tate nodded his acceptance and added, "I'ma hurryin' cuz I'm hungry!"

AFTER SUPPER THE YOUNG PEOPLE, Rachel, Hank, and Reuben who was now hobbling on a pair of crutches fashioned by Tate, went to the porch to sit and visit. Sean and Sadie were in the clearing with Lobo, playing one of their games of tag. The others were still at the table and deep in discussion when Hank hollered into the house, "Indians!"

Tate and Lex grabbed at their rifles standing by the door

and were on the porch before Hank returned to the other two young people. Because Lobo had not sounded a warning, Tate wasn't too concerned, but when he recognized their visitors, he quickly set his rifle down and descended the steps with a broad smile. "Raven, my friend. It is good to see you, and you've brought Red Blossom too!" He turned to call to the house, "Maggie! Feather! Come on out! It's Raven and Blossom!"

The two women were followed by Cora who stopped on the porch beside Lex and spoke softly to the trader, "Does he know every Indian in this country?"

"Pretty much. If he don't know 'em, they ain't worth knowin', or at least not worth bein' friends with, like them Apache that attacked the wagons, fer instance," answered the trader.

"So, whattaya think he's gonna do? 'Bout the wagons, I mean?"

"Dunno, but it ain't in him to turn down somebody needin' help. Even if he don't like 'em," replied Lex.

"So, Tate, muh friend, could you 'splain sumthin' to me? I mean, we had a nice peaceful country hyar and then them Ute hit Fort Pueblo, and it ain't been the same since. So, what's been goin' on?" asked Lex. Everyone was gathered on the porch and the steps, and they had been talking about the wagon train and the problems after the attack, and what might happen in the days ahead.

"Well, I'll do my best. You know about Fort Mass-achusetts, don't you?"

"You mean that so-called fort built in that mud hole on the side o' them mountains down yonder?"

Tate chuckled at Lex's description, "That's the one. Well, when they finally got it built, they moved in a couple companies o' Dragoons to make a show that it was no longer Mexican territory, but them troops kept runnin' off an' they never amounted to much an' most folks just paid no attention to the fort and the troops." He looked to Raven who grinned and nodded in agreement.

"But after that set-to last Christmas at Fort Pueblo, they got about five hundred more troops, volunteers mostly, to go after Chief Blanca and that bunch that hit the fort. Well, this spring, they purty much run 'em off, and then they split the troops. Carson guided 'bout half of 'em down Poncha Pass an' that's when they had another big fight in the valley of the Arkansas you heard 'bout."

"Yeah, that were just a couple months back weren't it?" asked the trader.

"Yup. That's right. And the other half of 'em went back th'other way and those that were left ain't been doin' much but tryin' to shore up the walls an' buildings. With last winter's snowfall, the fort's been a mess, and them soldiers ain't hardly left from behind the walls. That's why this bunch o' renegade bucs been rovin' around. They's 'bout all that's left o' the alliance 'tween the Jicarilla and the Mouache. An' now, after we whupped that bunch, wouldn't surprise me none if the chiefs start lookin' to make peace. But, can't be sure o' nuthin' nowadays."

"So, now that it 'peers the threat from the Mouache and Jicarilla seems to be over, what'cha gonna do 'bout them pilgrims," prodded the trader.

Tate looked at the man and shook his head and shrugged his shoulders. In any man's language, that meant he just didn't know.

CHAPTER TWENTY-SIX
CROSSING

His hands behind his head, Tate lay on his back staring at the rafters overhead. Maggie was on her side next to him, head on the pillow, as they talked softly of the decision to be made.

"You know, it's been some time since we visited my pa, and he's never seen Sadie. This might be a good time for a visit," she suggested.

He turned to look at his redhead and said, "That would be a long ride, especially for Sadie."

Maggie giggled, "Sadie is it? She's what's holding you back? That little lassie rides as well as any of us! She's more a part of her little paint than the spots on that horse's hide! Ha! She would see it as a grand adventure, and if you put a rifle in her hands, she'd show you a thing or two 'bout shootin', she would. She can already handle her bow as well as me!" She had the image of Sadie and her first ride circling in her mind. White Feather had come for a visit, she had a special fondness for Sadie, and had given her the name of Dancing Owl because of her inexhaustible energy and her wide eyes that took in everything. Feather had told Maggie of the way of her people and that youngsters would learn to ride even before they learned to walk, and that by the age of five summers, they were expected to handle any horse they were given. Maggie had been a little afraid, but with White Feather's guidance and constant encouragement, Sadie was soon handling the paint pony Feather had given her, and Maggie and Tate were both surprised and pleased at the child's proven ability.

"If we were to do this, it might be a long time before we come back home, maybe never," cautioned Tate.

"Don't you see, Tate? Our home is not this cabin, this place, our home is our family. Wherever we are together, that's where our home is, no matter if it's on top of a mountain or in a cabin in the woods, as long as we're together." She snuggled up close to her man to emphasize her point. He dropped his arm around her shoulders and pulled her closer.

He looked into her green eyes, smiled, and said, "I sure don't know how I was ever so lucky as to have a woman like you for my wife. You're an amazing woman, Maggie my girl."

She stretched up to plant a kiss on his lips, smiled at him, and said, "It's about time you realized that!" and giggled as he started tickling her and laughing together.

"Shhh, you'll wake ever'body up! This hotel is full o' folks tryin' to get their sleep," he admonished, but didn't let up on the tickling. It was their way of finishing all of their serious conversations, just showing each other their love and respect and happiness.

TATE SAT quiet on his bench beneath the big spruce, looking at the lazy moon that was losing its brightness as the sun started its climb to crest the eastern horizon and start another day. As was his practice, he would spend time with his Lord before making any change or big decision. The footsteps from behind he recognized as those of the trader, Lex. Tate spoke without turning, "Join me, won't you?"

The trader chuckled, a deep low rattle in his chest, and stepped forward to sit beside his friend. "I've always known there was sumpin' different 'boutchu, a kinda quiet peace, an' I figgered it was sumpin' like this. I often wisht I had that, but never knew how. Now, it's prob'ly too late fer an ornery ol' cuss like me."

Tate turned to look at his friend, saw a somber man with a heavy load of memories and regrets, but one that was still hopeful and with that faraway look in his eyes of a dreamer and wanderer, a searcher. "It's never too late, my friend." He looked through the trees and motioned with a sweep of his arm, "Do you really think the God that created all this, does his work by a timepiece or a calendar?"

Lex chuckled again, "No, I s'pose not. But I don't know much about things like that."

"That's why He made it so simple, so everyone could come to know Him. I was taught about it from my mother's knee and made my decision as a youngster, but I've known many that didn't understand or make that choice until later in life. The Bible talks about a thief on the cross beside Jesus that didn't make that choice until it was almost his last breath."

"Wal, just what is this hyar choice you're talkin' 'bout?" asked the wary mountain man.

Tate let a slow grin cross his face as he reached to the bench beside him and lifted his Bible, "Let me explain," and he began flipping through the pages to show his friend several passages of Scripture, most from the book of Romans.

"So, like I said, what you need to know is that you're a sinner, now you're not gonna give me any argument about that, are you?" asked Tate, grinning.

Lex looked at his friend with eyes that danced with mischief but curiosity as well, chuckled, and said, "Couldn't, even if I wanted to, you know me too well."

"Alright, and I showed you that we're all sinners and because of that, there's a penalty for sin, which is death and hell forever. You understand that, don't you?"

"Ummmhumm, seems right after all."

"But God sent His son Jesus to die on the cross to pay that penalty for us, so we wouldn't have to, unless we chose to, and when He did, He purchased the gift of eternal life which is ours if we but ask for it. You understand?"

"Uh, yeah, I think so. But that's what's so bafflin' to me, I cain't imagine anyone sacrificin' his own son fer a no-account like me!"

Tate let a chuckle escape as he explained, "Well, most folks have heard John 3:16, *For God so loved the world that he gave his only begotten son, that whosoever believeth in Him should not perish but have everlasting life.* You remember that, don't you?"

"Yeah, after muh pa died when them Pottawatomie Injuns attacked our place, Ma used to recite that ever night 'fore we went to bed. *Everlasting life.* Humm, that's what'chur talkin' 'bout, ain't it?"

"Yup, and to believe on Him, is to just take that step and ask for that gift of eternal life. Just a simple prayer, you know, ask Him to forgive your sins, give you the gift of eternal life, and like my momma always said, it's a good thing to say thanks for anything you get."

"I can do that. Would'ju pray with me?"

"Sure," answered Tate and the two friends sat side by side as the rising sun in the east brushed the western sky with a faint hint of pink to tell of the coming new day. And they spoke with the Creator from their hearts.

As they raised their heads, Lex took a deep breath that

lifted his shoulders and as he exhaled, he said, "Thanks, Tate. I needed that." He looked to the dim light that dusted the far mountains and asked, "So, what'cha gonna do? 'Bout them wagons, I mean."

"Well, I wanted to talk to you about that. Just what are you planning on doing? You mentioned going to California or something, didn't you?"

"Yeah, an' I been talkin' to that there Cora 'bout that too. Ya know, that woman's a purty good gunsmith an' a right fine woman, too!"

"What's that got to do with California?" asked Tate, suspecting there was more to what he was saying.

"Wal, we was talkin' 'bout how a tradin' post an' a gunsmith kinda work together, and then I was also thinkin' 'bout where would be good place. An' I thot 'bout a couple. You know how I been doin' purty good tradin' with Two Eagles and his people, I thot mebbe a post there at the place where ya' take off into the mountains fer Cochetopa pass, might be a good 'un. You know, with these wagon trains takin' the Old Spanish Trail north route to Californy, an' with the Ute gettin' more friendly with the white man, whatchu think?"

"Yeah, that might work. But you said you thought about a couple places, what's the other place?"

"You recomember a place called, Fort Uncompahgre? It was out in the flats where the Gunnison, or what they used to call the Grand, river and the Uncompahgre river come together. It was started by that Frenchman, what's his name, Rooba, somethin'. Ya know the place I'm talkin' 'bout?"

"Yeah, it was Antoine Robidoux that started it, and some others too. But I thought that was closed?"

"Yeah, but I reckon it wouldn't take much to get one a goin' again. What with bein' friendly with the Utes, and the wagons takin' this trail, might work. An' even if it didn't, we could allus go on to Californy!"

As they walked back into the clearing before the cabin, Tate saw Raven leading their horses from the corral and Red Blossom and White Feather on the porch with Maggie and Cora. The women were hugging and saying their goodbyes and White Feather dropped to one knee to give Sadie Marie, Dancing Owl, a big hug. There had always been a special connection between the two and they lingered together. When Tate came to Raven's side, he said, "It has been good to see my friend again," and the two men clasped forearms and drew each other close.

"You are my brother and your woman tells me it will be many moons, maybe summers, before we see you again," spoke Raven, somberly.

"That may be, but even if you are not here, you will always ride by our side."

White Feather approached and reached to give Tate a hug, then the two stepped back to look at one another, "You will always be my friend," said Feather, quietly.

"Yes," answered Tate, at a loss for words. He drew her close and hugged her again. Their friendship had been a part of his life since his first year in the mountains, but those that lived in the wilderness knew that with every parting, there might never be another meeting.

Maggie came to his side and the two stood, arms around each other's waist, as they bid goodbye to their friends. They watched as the three disappeared into the trees and Maggie asked, "Will there be any danger, just the three of them, and the Apache doing as they are?"

Tate laughed, "Those three are the match of any bunch o' renegades that would dare to come against them. Don't you remember, Feather and Blossom are proven warriors of the Comanche, they ain't just a couple o' women that can't defend themselves. Huhhuhn, they're better than most warriors of any band. They'll do a good job of protectin' Raven."

Maggie laughed at his comment, hugged him close and asked, "So, are we going to visit my pa?"

"I reckon, might as well. Don't want you gettin' bored just sittin' 'round the cabin, now do we?"

She smiled at her man as they walked together back to the cabin to get ready for the journey. There was much to do to prepare for this jaunt and time was slipping away. She tried not to let her excitement show, but she was anxious to prepare all that would be needed, and even more anxious to be on the trail again.

CHAPTER TWENTY-SEVEN
DECISION

THEY GATHERED AT THE TWO MOUNDS OF DIRT, COVERED BY rocks and marked with crudely fashioned crosses. Another day started with a brief funeral for the two victims of the attack from the young bucs of the Jicarilla and Mouache. Jesse Whitman read the Scripture and spoke the few words before the group sang a verse of "Footsteps of Angels" *They the holy one weakly, Who the cross of suffering bore, Folded their pale hands so meekly, Spake with us on earth no more.* Most just mouthed or mimicked the words, it being an unfamiliar song to most. With a last short prayer, the group moved away from the graves and gathered around the nearest wagon, which was Sidney Northrup's.

"Folks, there's some things we need to decide 'fore we move out from here. We need us a captain, what with both Harold and George gone now, an' we need to decide 'bout what we're gonna do. Now, most of ya heard what that buck-skin feller, Tate Saint, said 'bout not havin' enough to fight off another attack. An' he's right 'bout that, cuz near's I can figger, we got us seven men an' three scouts, an' if'n we get hit like we did yestiddy, well, . . ."

"But, what about California an' the gold?" asked Conrad Eichman, his wife Olga at his side and nodding her head. Their eleven-year-old, Adolf, was busy chasin' after a garter snake he found near the water.

"I think you all know how I feel about that, but gettin' ourselves kilt ain't gonna do nobody no good."

Heads nodded, and they looked around at each other until Lee Cutler spoke, "I don't like the idea of backtrackin' none, so what about goin' up to Fort Bridger an' joinin' up with another train?" Several spoke among themselves, discussing and commenting on the thought of the Oregon Trail and the safety of a larger train.

"Yeah, we could do that. But one o' them freighters we came out with said most o' the wagon trains goin' on the Oregon Trail are doin' just that, goin' to Oregon. An' we wanna go to California!"

"Do you think that mountain man's gonna agree to guide us?" asked Edna Garmin, standing beside her son. She had wiped her tears and stood as stoic as possible, after having just buried her husband.

"Well, if'n he does, it'll sure make things easier for us. He seems to know 'bout the Indians and the mountains an' such, and he and his friends sure saved our bacon yestiddy. But we won't know till we either see him or hear from him. He did say he'd let us know today."

Sidney saw there was still considerable discussion and no general agreement, so he suggested, "How 'bout some o' you fellers helpin' out with Mrs. Garmin. Since Frank Simpson lost his wife, the two o' them have agreed to combine their stuff an' travel together. Now, don't none of you start waggin' your tongues 'bout nothin'. It's just a matter of convenience for the both of 'em. But we could use some help sortin' things out amongst the stuff from both wagons. That'll give us all a little time to think about things and maybe decide."

He stepped down from the trunk he had been standing on and led the volunteers to the Simpson wagon. Everyone had agreed to re-pack their wagons, redistribute the weight, and tend to any repairs of the gear, while they waited to hear from the mountain man.

THE NOTE on the door of the cabin read, "This cabin belongs to the Saint family. If you need shelter, you're welcome to use it, but put things back the way you found them so the next person can use it too."

Maggie turned in her saddle for one last wistful look at their home. Memories flooded in and she let a few tears chase one another down her cheeks. She put on a brave face and turned with a smile and said, "Lead the way!"

Tate grinned and gigged his horse to the trail they used just the day before when they went to the aid of the wagons. It was quite a caravan, Tate and Maggie each led two pack-mules, with Sean riding beside his dad and Sadie alongside Maggie. They were followed by Reuben, with a re-adjusted and well-wrapped splint holding his leg out from the stirrup as he rode his bay gelding. Rachel rode side by side with Hank Greene, both on the spare horses that had served as pack-horses, from Tate's string. Cora rode a mule, and quite happy about it as she had more confidence in a deliberate thinking mule than an impulsive horse, and she led their string of three mules loaded with all their belongings. Lex Barkley followed with his long string of four pack-mules bringing up the rear. But they were an excited and happy group as each had thoughts about what their future might hold, some romantic, others adventurous, but all full of positive expectations.

The convoy of horses and mules coming from the trees

was more than what the people of the wagons were expecting, and several men grabbed for rifles as they gathered by the wagon nearest the approaching cavalcade. Sidney Northrup was the first to recognize Tate, "That's Tate Saint folks! You can put up your rifles, cuz they sure ain't Injuns!" There was a general chatter of relief and hopes that moved among the group as they stepped forward to welcome the visitors. But when they recognized Cora and family, and Hank Greene, there was shock, surprise and elation among the entire group. The men that made the decision to leave Hank behind and to not return for the Ritter's were both dead and it was mostly the women that raised the excitement level as several ran to greet Cora and the others.

Sidney Northrup and Lee Cutler walked to meet Tate and Sidney asked, "Does this mean you're gonna guide us?" He had a broad smile and a look of hopefulness in his eyes as he stood beside the mountain man's horse.

Tate looked around, approving of the attitude of the people as they welcomed Hank, Cora, and family. He motioned for Lex to come up and Tate swung down from his horse. He stood before the two men and said, "Well, we need to talk about that. It'd be best if we can get everybody together so any that have questions, we can get 'em answered, or try to, anyway."

"Sure, sure," answered Sidney, and raised his voice and his hand to get everyone's attention. "Folks, folks, listen up, please." He waited a few moments until he had everyone's attention. "Let's gather over yonder by that wagon," pointing at the nearest wagon, Eichman's, and said, "Mr. Saint wants to talk to us."

Tate gave a surprised look at Sidney, as he wasn't used to being addressed as Mr. Saint. He gave it a quick thought and realized that was probably the first time anyone had ever used the Mr. when talking to him. He just shook his head and grinned a little, tethered his horse to a nearby bit of greasewood and walked to the wagon. When everyone gathered around, he stood on the tongue of the wagon and looked at the people, "For those of you that didn't catch my name last time, I'm Tate Saint. That there," pointing to Maggie, "is my wife Maggie and those are my children, Sean and Sadie. I think you know those folks," motioning to Cora and family, "and that fella there is my good friend, Lex Barclay.

"We've talked about things, and I'm assuming that since you haven't moved either way, that you couldn't decide whether to go to Fort Bridger or back to Bent's Fort, like I suggested. Now, Lex there, is lookin' to set himself up a new tradin' post and he's thought about a couple places."

An impatient Fred Honeycutt interrupted, "What does that have to do with us goin' to California?"

Tate looked at the man and asked Northrup in a low voice, "What's that man's name?"

"Honeycutt, Fred. He's got a wife, couple o' boys that have been scoutin', and he's almighty anxious to get some gold, like the rest of us."

Tate lifted his eyes to the man, judging him by his demeanor and spoke again. "Well, let's get a few things settled right now. I'm not going to guide you all the way to California!" He paused as several of the folks began talking to one another and shuffling their feet as they looked around, and Tate continued, "But, Lex here might!" The mood changed again, as swiftly as their hopes had fallen, they lifted again, and they looked to the bearded mountain man that stood near Tate. "First off, is there anyone here that's a preacher, or somethin' like that?" He looked around at the upturned faces, several looked at the man that had conducted the funeral just a short while earlier, and Jesse Whitman slowly lifted his hand. "Good, then you can get folks hitched, am I right?"

Whitman nodded his head, but his brow was wrinkled in a question as he waited for Tate to say more.

"Since they've purty much agreed to be business partners, I thought they oughta get hitched proper, so Lex an' Cora need to get that fixed. Can you do that?" He looked at the man who nodded his head as a slow smile crossed his face. Tate looked to Lex and saw surprise and wonder written on his face as he held out his free hand, palm up and his head cocked to one side as he silently asked a question of his friend. This had not been discussed, but Tate smiled mischievously. The women looked to Cora who dropped her head, trying to hide a smile and Rachel put her hand on her mother's arm, smiling and stifling a giggle.

Rachel tugged on her mother, "I think we need to go get you ready for a wedding!"

Cora's face and neck were showing red as she looked at her daughter, "You think so?"

"Yes, I've seen the way you two have been looking at each other. I think it's a good thing."

"And I've seen the way you and that boy have been lookin' at each other. You know you're too young to be havin' those kinda thoughts, don'tchu?"

"What kinda thoughts?" asked Rachel, demurely, smiling at her ma.

"Don't give me that! You know what I'ma sayin'," scolded her mother. The two were walking arm in arm back to the wagon and stopped to look to one another.

"Ma, we've been talking about it, but we both agree we're still a little too young. But, maybe after we get settled in California and he gets a job or mine or whatever, then we'll get married." Cora started to interrupt, but Rachel held up her hand, "Now's not the time to talk about it. 'Sides, it's already settled," she tugged at her mother's arm to start to the wagon, "but right now, we need to get you ready for your own wedding!"

TATE CONTINUED AS if what he had said was nothing more than a simple observation that everyone would understand. "Now, we'll head across the valley, toward that cut in the mountains yonder," he pointed to the foothills of the San Juans to the west, "that's where the Cochetopa Pass cuts down through the mountains and comes out in the valley of the Gunnison River. It used to be called the Grand, but since Captain Gunnison made a couple forays down thisaway, they changed the name to Gunnison. Now, this here," he pointed to the trail they had been following, "is the Old Spanish Trail, the north branch of it, and it will take you to California. If'n you survive it, that is. And Lex there was considering settin' up a tradin' post o'er yonder by them foothills, or goin' on to the valley of the Gunnison and west to where Fort Uncompahgre was and settin' up a new tradin' post there.

"Now, what that means to you is, he can guide you just as good as I can, prob'ly better, cuz he's been there before an' I ain't."

"But if he decides to set up a post, what happens to us?" asked Fred Honeycutt.

"Well, he's agreed that whatever he decides, he'll still guide you as far as Fort Uncompahgre. What with so many folks goin' to California, you'll probably meet up with other wagons 'tween here an' there and make it safer for all. But at least he'll get you a lot closer than you are now."

"What are you gonna do?" added Honeycutt.

"Me'n my family'll see you at least across the valley here, maybe even down the Cochetopa, then we got other places to go." He paused as everyone took in what had been said, when he thought they had understood, he continued, "Now, we got a lotta light left an' it's gonna take at least two days just to get across the valley to them mountains yonder. And another four or five days to get down the Cochetopa. So, long as I'm guidin' you will do what I say, when I say it, no questions asked. Cuz, if you stop to ask questions, that just might be 'nuff time for some warrior lookin' for honors to separate you from your scalp and you won't be askin' any more questions. Understand?"

He looked around the group nodding their heads and then looked to Sidney, "Alright then," he said speaking softly to Sidney, "since you're the newly elected Captain, let's get these folks to movin'. We can have that weddin' when we stop this evenin'."

Northrup nodded as he grinned, extended his hand to shake and said, "Thank you. I sure am glad to have you with us. I really had no idea what to do, but now I'm relieved and very grateful."

Tate smiled, shook his hand, and moved away to fetch his horse and gather up his brood. Lex looked at him and asked, "How'd you know?"

Tate chuckled and answered, "Everybody knew, it was as obvious as that sun in the sky, you were just hidin' in the shade and didn't want to admit it. But, let me be the first to congratulate you, then you need to go talk to your bride! Oh, and by the way, your new daughter and that young man, Michael, might be getting ready to do the very same thing!"

Lex turned abruptly to look at his friend, mouth agape, "Whatchu mean?!"

"I mean, you might be a grandfather before you know it!"

Lex stared at Tate, and a smile began to cross his face as he thought about what had been said. He remembered the many times he had pictured himself sitting in a rocker by a warm fire with a fine woman nearby and children playing at his feet, a dream he had thought was gone forever. But now, that might mean grandchildren and that was alright too.

CHAPTER TWENTY-EIGHT
SAGUACHE

"You fellas stay out about two miles ahead, an' there ain't much to see in these flats, but I want'chu to be watchin' for two things. First, keep your eyes on the skyline for any fine trails o' smoke, that's 'bout all you're gonna see of any Indians. Now, we're headin' straight across toward that notch in them hills yonder, it'll take us a couple days. And then I want'chu to ride easy, them flats out there are loaded with all sorts o' things that'll spook your horse. Jackrabbits, coyotes, an' worst of all, rattlesnakes. So, sit deep, an' be watchful."

Matthew and Luke Honeycutt answered in unison, "Yessir!" reined around and rode off to lead the way. The San Luis Valley sloped to the lowest point in the bottom of the valley where the San Luis Creek accepted the runoff waters from the mountains and in a wet summer would carry it all the way to the Rio Grande, but this wasn't one of those wet summers. The bottom of the valley was marked by the white of alkali with the only vegetation being various forms of cacti. Cholla, prickly pear, hedgehog, and other cacti dug deep into the adobe and alkali to find any moisture, while the stunted sage and greasewood struggled to catch any moisture that fell. Random patches of buffalo grass showed only by the pale yellowish-brown moustaches they made on the frowning face of the flats.

By the end of the first day, wagons and mules alike had taken on a ghostly appearance with the dust of the white alkali painting everything that moved. Tate had cautioned the pilgrims to have full water barrels and anything else that could hold water as the dusty valley bottom desert would yield no moisture for the travelers.

By the time the wagons circled for the end of the day's travel, the pilgrims knew exactly what Tate had warned them about. Although they saw snow-capped peaks behind them and green hills and mountains before them, where they were was drier than last week's flour biscuits, and almost as hard. Every time they put a foot down, white dust puffed up and circled around before settling. Their faces showed lines of white mud where eyes watered trying to cleanse themselves, and the sweat around their collars became stiff and white. Every breath elicited a cough, and sputum, and snot showed white.

The tired and dirty waggoneers trudged to the fires, holding out tin plates and cups with thin coatings of white dust. Reuben Ritter lifted his coffee cup but saw a thin film of white floating and tossed the coffee aside. "Ain't there nuthin' that ain't got alkali on it?"

"Aww, it ain't that bad, just close your eyes an' you prob'ly won't even taste it," declared Cora as she handed Reuben his tin plate with deer meat, potatoes, and gravy, all looking a little on the white side. He wrinkled his nose but picked up the fork and went to work. The people had all gathered around before they broke for supper and had the wedding. Cora looked at Lex and smiled and said, "Well, at least muh weddin' clothes were white!" and chuckled.

Lex lifted his eyes and smiled between bites and said, "Yup, they was. Almost as white as my beard."

Cora giggled and said, "Rachel asked me if I was marryin' Santa Claus!"

Lex feigned insult and said, "Now, hol' on thar, I ain't that old! It's the alkali!"

Rachel and Reuben were both laughing, and she chimed in with, "Are you sure?"

Everyone enjoyed the relief of levity and continued eating. "So, do we call you Pa or Lex or what?" asked Reuben. He grinned at Lex and Cora, now sitting beside one another on the bench beside the fire.

"With cookin' like this, you can even call me Santa Claus, just don't call me late for supper!" declared Lex as he leaned against Cora.

THE SECOND DAY'S travel across the valley started on a high note with a promise from Tate that everyone would have ample fresh water and could take a bath in Saguache Creek. Although the bottom of the valley was deep with alkali, patches of greasewood and rabbitbrush with clumps of buffalo grass began to show as they drove with the sun at their backs. The Cutler wagon had rotated into the lead and the Honeycutt brothers took over the reuda of mules and horses. With the mules from the O'Toole, Greene, and Garmin wagons, plus the few spares already, and the few horses that were only occasionally ridden, the remuda required constant attention. With the brothers tending the horses and mules, scouting duties were handled by Hank Greene and Michael Garmin.

They were less than an hour on their way when Hank Greene rode back to report to Tate, "Did you see that smoke yonder, just beyond that point?"

"Yeah, I'm thinkin' the Ute's might be camped there. Just keep a sharp lookout, an' don't go beyond that point. Wait for us to catch up an' I might take a look see. If it's who I think it is, we won't be in any danger."

Hank nodded his understanding and reined around to depart at a canter to catch up with Michael Garmin. After delivering the word from Tate, Hank asked, "What're you an' your ma gonna do? Still look for gold?"

"I dunno, but I don't know what else we'd do. Only thing we done back in Missouri was to farm, an' I ain't wantin' to do no farmin'. I'd rather try gold minin' first. But, we ain't got much in the way of money. Pa had figgered on gettin' a job in a mine or sumpthin' till we got settled in a place of our own or got a claim of our own. So, I dunno, really. What about'chu?"

Hank looked at his friend and said, "I ain't sure neither. The Ritter's, or the Barclay's now, they offered for me to stay with them, but . . . I just dunno."

"Hey, maybe we could get us a claim together. With both of us workin' one, we might get it to pay off real quick!" answered Michael, enthusiastically.

"Do you know anything about minin' gold?" asked Hank.

Michael's excitement waned quickly as he dropped his head, "No, I don't. You?"

"I ain't even seen any gold, much less know how to find it. But maybe we can get a job in a mine and learn! Can't be that hard with so many doin' it!"

"It ain't the doin', it's the findin' that's hard," declared Michael, his enthusiasm taking another dip.

"So, if we're all goin' together," began Hank, thinking about Rachel, "which one of us is gonna end up with Rachel?"

Michael stopped and looked at his friend, "Don't tell me she's got you . . . you know, interested?"

"Wal, I thought about it, but all she can talk about is you! So, I reckon that means, I dunno, what about you?"

"That's why I was hopin' we could work together and both of us make enough to start our own place, or mine, or whatever. I've been wantin' to ask her to marry me, but not 'til I could take care of her, proper like, you know. We've talked about it and she wants to, but we both know we need to be settled into some kinda life with a future. But since my pa died, I need to make sure ma's gonna be alright. I reckon she could live with us after, you know, after we get married, but . . ."

"Well my friend, I'm sure things'll work out. Rachel's a mighty fine girl and anybody'd be mighty lucky to have her for a wife."

The two friends rode together, both letting their minds wander into an uncertain future, but a future full of hopes and dreams. They were watchful, but quiet, as the responsibilities of adulthood pushed into their consciousness.

THE WAGONS WERE WELL BACK from the scouts, and Tate and company rode alongside with the many pack animals trailing. Most riders and pilgrims had scarves over their noses and mouths, hat brims turned down low, collars up, all to keep out some of the penetrating and bitter alkali dust. Many of the wagon drivers were bored and nodding as the wearisome plodding of the mules, constant creak of the wagons, and rattle of trace chains lulled them into an almost catatonic state. Tate stood in his stirrups and shaded his eyes to look toward the green hills and was startled, dropping him back in his seat, and grabbing the reins tight, when the lead mules brayed and reared up, pawing at the air. When the mules dropped to all fours, they took off at a dead run, Lee Cutler rearing back on the reins and shouting at run-away mules, "Whooaa, Whooaa you crazy mules! Whoa!" Marilyn Cutler could be heard screaming as the wagon stormed away from the rest of the train, astonishing the other mule tenders into pulling up on their teams. The alkali and adobe dust billowed behind the wagon, obscuring it from sight, but the screams of the woman could still be heard.

Tate dropped the lead to his pack-mule, hollered at Maggie as he motioned to the mule, "Get it!" and dug his heels into Shady's ribs as horse, wolf, and man kicked dust to start their pursuit. Lex mirrored Tate and took off after his friend. It was hard and dangerous to give chase into the dust cloud, in this country where it was common to have prairie dog villages with hundreds of holes and mounds that would break the leg of a horse and upend mount and rider, it was foolish to make the chase at an all-out gallop, but lives were in danger and they had to risk it. Tate swerved to the side to get a clearer view, saw the wagon still bouncing across the rugged flats and leaned down to urge his horse faster. He felt the surge of response from the grulla and slapped his neck in reassurance, spoke into the horse's ear, "Let's get 'em, Shady boy!"

As he came alongside the lead mule that was running all out, ears laid back and teeth bared with nostrils flaring, eyes wide and scared, Tate leaned down to grab the headstall and lean back against the straining mule. The mule's eyes turned to this new threat, but seeing a man, he began to respond, and Tate could feel the pace of the animal slow. When the lead mule began to slow, the others felt it, and began to respond. Tate didn't let up but leaned back, pulling the animal's head up even higher, and the mule began to dig in his heels, dropped his rump, slid, hopped, slid again and the team finally slowed to a walk and came to a stop.

Tate released his grip on the harness, turned back to Cutler and saw the man and woman, holding tight to one another. He heard the sobs of Marilyn, muffled against her husband's shoulder and Tate said, somewhat softly, "In a hurry, were you?"

Cutler released his wife and looked at Tate, sighed heavily, and said, "No, it was the biggest rattlesnake I ever saw! He struck at the lead mule there, mighta got him, but that's what spooked 'em, and once they took off, I couldn't stop 'em. Thanks, thanks for stoppin' 'em for us. If you hadn't done that, there's no tellin' where we'd ended up. Thanks."

Tate looked across the mules, saw Lex, and knew he had done the same thing on that side. "Thanks Lex, glad you made it. I was afraid to pull on 'em too hard, didn't wanna make 'em take a quick turn an' spill the wagon. But when I saw you, I knew we could do it together. Thanks!" Lex lifted his head in a nod and both men turned back to get their wives. Tate called to Cutler, "Go ahead an' step down, let them animals have a drink. The other'sll catch up soon 'nuff."

Tate pulled beside Lex and looked around. "How 'bout you bringin' the rest of 'em along, I think I'll go ahead a ways. If I'm right, I'm thinkin' Two Eagles might be camped up yonder, round that bend. If it's them, we can camp along the creek an' be alright, but if not, well . . . "

Lex grinned and nodded. Tate reined around and started for the green hills. The two scouts were sitting their mounts, looking back at the wagons and the settling dust from the runaway and saw Tate and Lobo approaching. "You fellas wait here, I'm goin' up to that point and see what that smoke is all about. If you see me come runnin' back, you light out for the wagons and warn 'em."

"Warn 'em of what?" asked Hank.

"Indians, what else," answered Tate and started for the point.

HANK GREENE CAME RIDING BACK TO THE WAGONS AT A gallop. Waving his hat in the air and shouting, making everyone think they were under another Indian attack. But as he slid to a stop beside Lex and his string of mules, he was smiling broadly and said, "Durndest thing I ever did see! Water, shootin' up right outta the ground!" He was waving back to the direction he came from and added, "There's a pond there an' a stream runnin' outta it, but the water's just bubblin' up like I ain't never seen!"

Lex relaxed, sat back in his saddle grinning, and looked at the younker and said, "Yup, there's a few of 'em here," waving his arm around, "they be called artesian. Artesian wells or springs, good water too." He waved the wagons to follow and said, "We'll let everybody hole up by that pond you spoke of, at least till Tate gets back. Good a place as any! So, lead the way young'un, go 'head on!" he directed as he jerked on the lead rope of his mule string. Cora came alongside and said, "What'd you call it? Ar . . .ar . . what?"

"Artesian. Don't know where the word comes from, French I think. But there's a few of 'em 'round this area.

Usually, ya just find little springs, an' them mostly in the mountains, water comin' outta the rock, but these are bigger, and come right up from the ground. It's a sight. Now, Tate says he seen some farther up north, that make these look mighty little, says the water shoots up higher'n them trees. Ain't never seen it muh own self, but I ain't never known the boy to lie none, neither. But as he'd say, Ain't God somethin'?" They rode together and talked, Lex telling more about the country and life in the mountains. He chuckled as he thought, "Not too far from here, there's some springs with hot water, I mean boilin' hot! They's a bit of a pond there, a deep pool, an' it's a fine place to sit'n soak, get the kinks out. Injuns like it too, an' there's kinda understandin' 'mongst folks here'bouts, that when they're at them springs an' soakin', wal, it's kinda whatcha call neutral territory. Nobody makes war there, ever'body's at peace with one 'nother. Now, after they gets out an' dries off, then it's Johnny git'chur gun!"

Cora looked at Lex and answered, "Like you said, this here's some mighty fine country. I been learnin' a lot, and the more I see, even the strange things, the more I like it."

Lex looked at his new bride and smiled, "That there's music to muh ears, yessir, music!"

TATE KNEW THIS COUNTRY, had hunted here before and visited the Ute band of his friend Two Eagles. This valley of the Saguache Creek and the beginning of Cochetopa Pass was a winter grazing ground for elk herds that came down from the higher mountains but needed a sheltered valley with ample graze. With the larger creek fed by the runoff creeks from the surrounding hills, the valley yielded ample graze of buffalo grass and grama, both favorite foods of deer and elk.

The point of land that marked the beginning of the

Cochetopa pass valley was a larger finger of hills that tumbled from the taller San Juans, farther back and higher up. Three small fingers came from the larger ridge and Tate followed the wide draw that pointed toward the high point of the ridge that overlooked the valley beyond. This cut back formed a preferred camp for a large band of Indians that always sought a location that afforded protection, water, and graze for their animals.

With little vegetation on the ridge save for a few stunted pinyon and gnarled cedar, Tate ground-tied Shady and with Lobo at his side, he hunkered down and worked his way to the ridge. Knowing he couldn't silhouette himself on the skyline, he bellied down and with Lobo also crawling on his belly, the two compatriots lifted their heads just enough to eyeball the valley below. Where Tate expected to see as many as a hundred tipis or lodges of the Ute, there was not a single hide lodge. No Indians, no horse herd, no children playing with their hoops. None of what he had anticipated lay in the valley below. But he immediately saw the source of the earlier smoke.

Arrayed in a circle that enclosed several campfires, were thirteen prairie schooner wagons. Canvas bonnets arched to catch the afternoon's sun, a few people busy with simple tasks, but no order to the movement. Tate scanned the hill-sides for any sign of an outpost or anyone on guard, but there was none. The people below appeared listless, inactive, and as he watched he saw a woman carrying a bucket, stumble and fall, unnoticed by anyone among the wagons. As he looked closer with the benefit of his telescope, he saw several in bedrolls under the wagons, and tended to by a few others still active. He moved his scope around, searching the entire encampment and finally located what he suspected. A graveyard with a few crude crosses and several mounds of dirt, most still dark from freshly turned soil.

He spoke quietly to Lobo, "These people are sick, most likely cholera. Where them wagons are sittin' an' the flow o' that creek, they ain't been too particular 'bout their drinkin' water." He crabbed back from the crest and quickly snatched up the reins and swung aboard Shady. He looked to Lobo and said, "Let's go check on these folks, boy."

He dropped off the hills into the flats at a canter, rounded the point of land, and slowed to a trot as he neared the wagons. He expected at least a warning, but his approach went almost unnoticed by the people until a young man raised his hand to halt Tate and walked toward the visitor. The lad spoke with authority as he questioned, "Who're you and what'chu want?"

Tate sat relaxed in his saddle, both hands on the horn, and looked at the young man, "My name's Tate, and it looks like you folks have a problem."

"That's right, an' if you don't wanna get the blue death, you'll skedaddle."

"Blue Death? That's what some folks call cholera. Is that the problem?" asked Tate.

"Yup, first one's came down with it three days ago, buried six so far and more are likely to be gone soon," the authority of his voice was replaced by despair, even fear.

"Who's in charge?" asked Tate.

"Nobody, not since our wagonmaster and his men high-tailed it. They rode outta here right after the first one came down sick."

Tate breathed deep, and looked at the boy, "Well, looks like we got us some work cut out for us. I've got several wagons headed this way, so I'm gonna go stop them and get us some help. In the meantime, you make everybody empty out their water buckets and such and stop drinking the water, at least till we get back. That's why you're all gettin' sick!" He reined around and called back over his shoulder,

"I'll be back shortly! Take care o' that water!" He slapped his legs against Shady and took off at a gallop back to the wagons.

THE WAGONS WERE CLUSTERED about the pond with the artesian water, but when Lex saw Tate coming at a gallop, he shouted, "Head's up! Tate's a comin' at a run, looks like trouble!" The men scrambled for their rifles and the women gathered the few children and took cover behind the wagons. Tate slid to a stop and said, "It's alright folks! No danger! But I need you to gather 'round, got somethin' to say!" He walked to the end of one wagon and dropped the tailgate, hopped up on it and stood to await the others. Once they were around, he started, "Up yonder just a little ways, there's another wagon train!" The crowd looked to one another, excitedly. This is what they hoped for, more wagons and people to travel with for each other's safety. But they looked back to see an expression of concern on Tate's face and they quieted to listen. "They have a problem. There's some of 'em come down with cholera." The word whipped through the crowd like a cold winter wind, causing the women to pull their shawls about them and men to pull their families close. "But, they need help. Now, folks've found out a lot about cholera in the last few years and most believe it's caused by the water. But others say it's from water that's been tainted by people an' their ways. This bunch don't seem to know that an' their wagonmaster an' his crew have already run off an' left 'em. Now, I want you all to stay here, an' Lex, you know what they need to do 'bout campin' and water'n such. But, I need some to come help me tend to these folks. I know my woman, Maggie, will be comin' with me, but Rachel, if I could ask you to tend to Sean and Sadie while we're gone, that'd help." He looked to girl and she eagerly nodded her head.

Before Tate could continue, Cora stepped beside him and spoke up, "Folks, I know 'bout cholera. My folks died of it a few years back when St. Louis had it so bad. But I learnt about it, an' I'm gonna go help. We can get these folks better, but it'll take some work. An' if Tate don't mind, I'd like to take charge cuz I know purty much all ya' need to know 'bout fightin' it." She looked up at Tate and he nodded in agreement. He reached down and gave her a hand up to the tailgate.

She started, "There's some things we need. First off, we need some o' you to gather several o' them water barrels and fill 'em with this here fresh water an' load 'em on a wagon to take over there. Then we need some kerosene, we're gonna be burnin' some stuff, and we need some folks willin' to scrub an' clean, and others to do some buryin'." Cora didn't know what to expect, after all, these were the same people that turned their back on her and her family and left them behind. But she had seen a change in their attitude and demeanor, the change that comes from hardships endured together, and she was hopeful. She was not disappointed as several stepped to the tasks and within a short while, the small group of willing helpers were lined up behind Tate and they started to the people in need.

CHAPTER THIRTY
COCHETOPA

She was like a commander of the army of volunteers. Barking orders, directing workers, suggesting changes, all without hesitation but done in a way that the helpers willingly accepted and responded. It was immediately evident that Cora knew what was needed and didn't hesitate to require what was necessary from everyone. Lex and Hank had been sent on a hunting mission for fresh meat, Tate organized the water supply and the arrangement of the camp and animals to ensure the streams water was not polluted by human or animal waste. He made sure the water was clean for two days before using any for their purposes. The Honeycutt brothers were in charge of burning anything and everything that had been tainted or touched by any of the victims, and Ethel Northrup took charge of the women that scrubbed the pots, pans, and wagons of those that had been infected.

The change could be seen almost immediately. Those that had not been inflicted with the 'Blue Death' had their spirits lifted and began to work alongside those that had come to help. Within the first couple of days, there was activity and even laughter, as some of those that had been in fear of death began to smile and think of the future. Campfires blazed with fresh deer steaks dripping juices into the fires, cookpots with fine smelling stews boiled, and everything began to take on an order that showed concern and well-being. Although several were still frail and had the pall of death upon them, they would still manage a smile as others tended to their needs, keeping them and their surroundings clean and fresh.

It had been proven in the recent years that unsanitary conditions were the cause of the plague. With cities drawing drinking water from the same lakes that were used as dumps for refuse, it was the perpetuation of the infection that was rightfully blamed for the thousands of deaths. When people were given clean water, often fortified with salt, and other nourishment, they would regain their strength and health. Wagon trains that had taken drinking water downstream from the bushes where people relieved themselves and animals were grazing had unintentionally been infected. But when Tate and Cora took over, everything was changed, and people learned first-hand how to ensure their safety when it came to something as simple as drinking water.

It was all of a week before Tate had their wagons join the others by the Saguache Creek. But a camaraderie had already been established and people of both groups had become friends. As often happens in times of trial and challenge, people of different backgrounds and interests find the common bond of need and helping, and friendships are formed. Although there were a few that were still not fully recovered, everyone agreed that it was a time for celebration. There were a couple of fiddle players among the new group and Fred Honeycutt brought out his banjo and the crowd was soon singing and dancing for the first time in months.

Tate was sitting with Maggie as they clapped along with the others. They had taken a couple of turns dancing, and now rested and enjoyed the fun of the others. Alfred Mays,

Marilyn Cutler's brother and the man in charge of the scouts, stepped to Tate's side and said, "There's a group of about four or five Indians that have been watching us from the other side of the creek. I think they're coming over now," and nodded his head toward the brush by the creek that could barely be seen in the dwindling twilight. Mays had stationed the Honeycutt brothers and Hank Greene along the side of the wagons facing the creek and they now stood, rifles ready, as they watched the Indians approach. None of the Indians held their weapons ready, they appeared peaceful and the scouts had been cautioned about the friendly Utes. Tate and Maggie stood from the bench and started toward the Indians, not wanting to alarm the dancers, and within the first few steps, Tate recognized the two in the lead. "Lean Bear! Spotted Wolf! Welcome my friends." He stepped toward them, hand extended and clasped forearms with each man.

"Longbow! We recognized you and came to greet you. But why are you with all these?" he motioned to the wagons and the people.

Tate looked around and said, "Some of these people have been sick and we have helped them. They will be leaving soon. Is Two Eagles with you?"

"No, he is at our village. His woman has a new son and our people have chosen a new winter camp. We will be moving soon. We," he motioned to those with him, "are on a hunt for meat."

"Is your village camped far from here? We would like to see this new son of Two Eagles," asked Tate, bringing a grin to the face of the Ute.

"We are far to the south in the mountains. Two, three days ride," answered Lean Bear.

Tate looked at Maggie and back to Lean Bear and replied, "We are going north to see the father of Morning Sky. Tell

Two Eagles will we come see him when we return so he can show his new son. Will you join us for some food?"

"We have had our meal, we will return to our camp and ready for our hunt. May the Great Spirit watch over you," said Lean Bear as he turned to leave.

"And you as well, my friend."

They watched the Ute leave and realized the music had stopped and when they turned, they were surprised to see many of the people standing behind them and watching as the Utes left. Cora stepped forward and turned back to face the others, "See folks, it's like I said. He seems to know ever' Indian in these mountains by name and calls 'em all friends. We've learned a lot from this man." The crowd looked at Tate and Maggie and to one another as the talk among friends was soon replaced with calls for more music.

As the celebration began to wane, Tate and several of the men from both groups gathered around a fire and began to discuss what should be done in the coming days. "Folks, the way I see it is you all are wantin' to go to California, and you're on the north branch of the Old Spanish Trail that leads there, so, seems to me the logical thing is to go!" He chuckled as he watched their faces as if they had just realized the simplicity of what he was saying.

"Are you gonna guide us?" asked Sidney Northrup, hopefully.

"Well, Sidney, I have no interest in California, and you really don't need me. Lex here is a very capable man and he's already agreed to at least see you folks well on your way, if not all the way."

The people of the new group had been well impressed with both Cora and Lex as they helped their people during the crisis and they were pleased that Lex would guide them.

But those of the original group were hopeful they could convince Tate to stay with them. Lee Cutler detected the divided loyalties and spoke up, "Well, Tate, you've helped us more than we deserve, and we couldn't have made it this far without that help, but we also know that Lex was helping just as much. And if you have confidence in him, then we do too." He looked to the others for their agreement and was met with smiles and nodding heads.

"I'm mighty pleased to hear that. Maggie and I were plannin' on goin' north from here to go visit her pa that lives up in the Bayou Salado. It's been a few years since we seen him, and he's never seen his newest grandchild, so it's about time.

"We've enjoyed meeting and getting to know you folks, and we will keep you in our prayers as you travel. But, don't get your hopes set on finding gold, if you come across a likely place for a home and where you can raise a family, don't let the dream of riches keep you from makin' a good life for yourself. It takes more'n gold to make a happy family. I've known a lot o' happy folks that never saw a single gold nugget and didn't want to, cuz what they had was more valuable than any amount o' gold."But enough o' that preachin', let's all turn in and get ready for a new day when that sun comes o'er them mountains yonder!" His suggestion was met with several "amens" and "yessirs" as the crowd dispersed to their wagons.

Maggie took Tate's hand as they walked back to their camp and the two looked up at the star filled sky and Maggie said, "I love you, Tate Saint!"

He chuckled and put his arm around his bride and pulled her close and looked to her uplifted green eyes, saw the reflected sparkle of the stars, and said, "And I love you, Maggie O'Shaunessy Saint!" They kissed and held each other in the moonlight for a while but soon found their bedrolls beside their two youngsters and turned in for the night.

THERE WAS JUST A HINT OF FIRST LIGHT WHEN TATE WALKED down from the hillside toward the circled wagons. Now there were eighteen wagons, one to be left behind and one taken by Cora. The previous owners of those two wagons were buried with the other victims in the small graveyard at the edge of the hillside. With the gunsmithing gear of Cora and the trade goods of Lex, it was easier to haul them in a wagon than the extended mule train. As Tate walked to the edge of the circle where he had tethered their horses and mules, Maggie stepped around and welcomed him, "I'll get Sean and Sadie up now, we'll be ready in just a few moments." Tate nodded and walked to the campfire of Sidney Northrup, where Cora and Lex waited, coffee in hand.

It was a short goodbye among friends and Tate said to Lex, "I know these folks are in good hands, my friend. But once you get settled, drop us a line and let us know how you're doin', probably to Fort Bridger, that's not too far from my other cabin in the Wind River mountains."

"We'll do that, I'm certain shore that Cora can write'chu, I never learned muh own self, but she can!" he nodded as he spoke. Then he turned serious, and said, "I wanna thank you Tate, cuz if'n it weren't fer you, I'da never got up the nerve to say nuthin' to that woman. You been a good friend and I'ma thankin' you!"

Tate grinned and shook his friend's hand, and when Maggie released Cora, Tate gave her a hug and said to Reuben and Rachel, "You two take good care o' them two, understand?"

Both the young people nodded, grinned at Tate and Maggie and said, "We will."

Maggie gave Rachel a big hug and whispered in her ear, "And you take care of that young man, too."

Rachel pulled back and looked at Maggie, surprised, but smiling and nodded her head. "I'm sure the two of you will be very happy together. I have found, that a love that is born in times of trials and hardships, usually grows to become the strongest kind."

"Thank you, Maggie. Thank you," answered Rachel, tears beginning to trail down her cheeks. The two embraced again and Maggie pulled away to step aboard her buckskin.

Tate and Maggie were mounted, lead ropes to the pack-mules in hand, and Sean and Sadie were mounted and ready to go, excitement blazing in their eyes. With a last spoken goodbye, they turned their mounts to move off to the north east for the trail that would take them down Poncha Pass and into the valley of the Arkansas. As they started away, all four turned around in their saddles and waved at their friends. Those standing and watching returned the wave and a few of the women daubed small handkerchiefs at their eyes and turned away to get themselves ready for their journey.

WHEN DUSK SETTLED over them at the end of their second day, they rode from the mountains to make camp by the little river branch of the Arkansas. They were not in a hurry, as they knew they were within a short week of the Bayou Salado. The morning of the third day, Sean woke his father with a foot on his shoulder and when he stirred, Sean whispered, "Pa, there's some deer down by the water. Can I take one with my bow?"

Tate groaned but rolled from his covers, pulled on his high-topped moccasins, and walked to their packs to get his quiver and bow. With a nod to his son, he let Sean lead the way to the brush beside the river. He watched as Sean started his stalk, carefully placing each step, keeping his eyes on the brush that he suspected hid the deer, and Tate followed. The boy had learned well, lifting each foot and putting it down, toes first, soundlessly, always steady on his feet and with an arrow nocked on his bow. As they entered the brush, Sean slowly moved aside each branch, making certain nothing rubbed against his buckskin, nor whipped back to make a sound, and he peered through the thinner brush to spot his target. Three deer, two does and a young buck, had come to water and were standing with front feet at the edge of the water on the sandbank and two drank while the other watched. When the does had drunk their fill, they stepped back toward the brush, seeming to tip toe, and the buck dropped his head to the water. When the buck's eyes were down, Sean stepped into his bow, brought the arrow to full draw and let it fly to its mark. The arrow struck just behind the shoulder, low down, and pierced the rib cage, instantly felling the buck and startling the does to take flight. The buck stirred just once, kicked a leg, and lay still.

Sean turned back to his Pa and said, "How's that, Pa?"

"Mighty fine shooting, son. And you did your stalk very well. You're a fine hunter."

Sean seemed to swell with the praise from his father, and the two walked to the buck to begin the work of taking the meat. The rest of the day was spent as a family, building drying racks, smoking the meat, enjoying the time together. Tate sat at the fire, watching the youngsters help their mother, dropped his hand to Lobo and said, "You know boy, this is a mighty fine life, don'tchu think?" The big wolf looked up at the man and Tate was certain the canine was smiling as he stroked his hand across the scruffy neck.

Maggie walked over to sit beside Tate and watched the youngsters string the thin sliced deer meat onto the drying racks and said, "You know something? I think I've got you figured out. You're just a romantic at heart."

Tate scowled at looked at his wife, "What'chu mean?"

"The way you got Lex and Cora together. I heard him say if you hadn't done that, he never woulda got up the nerve. And others, like my Pa and Little Otter, and that man, what was his name, Knuckles? Seems like wherever you go, you get folks together. You're just the matchmaker of the mountains, that's what you are," she laughed and punched him on the shoulder.

He grinned and reached out to draw her near, "The only match I care about is you and me!"

FOUR MORE DAYS of travel and as the long shadows stretched across the flats of the Bayou Salado, they rounded the timbered knob of a hill and saw the isolated black mountain across the south fork of the South Platte river. Maggie had waited breathlessly to see some sign of the summer encampment of the Yamparika Ute and her first sight of a hide lodge brought a wide smile. Her father, Michael Patrick O'Shaughnessy, and his wife, Little Otter of the Yamparika made their home with her people. The two would occasionally make forays into the mountains to do a little prospecting, but that was only to make him feel he hadn't given up on his dreams. But the gold he had already found weighed heavy in their packs and he didn't really need any more, but the searching was his purpose.

When Maggie spotted the village, she turned to Tate and said, "I'm so excited, I can't hardly stand it!"

Tate chuckled and said, "I've an idea. We know which lodge is theirs, right?"

"Yeah, why?" she looked at her man questioningly and saw the mischievous glint in his eyes and said, "What?"

He outlined his plan as they rode nearer and said, "Now if we can just keep the scouts from spreading the word we're here."

MICHAEL LAY BACK against the braided willow backrest, carving on a wooden spoon for his wife, idly passing the time as she stirred the goodness in the pot hanging over the fire. He looked up when there appeared some minor commotion at the edge of the camp but returned to his whittling and paid little attention. When two little hands came from behind him and covered his eyes, he was startled, but not alarmed as he often enjoyed playing with the youngsters in the village who called him 'Uncle,' but these hands were different, lighter. A little voice came from behind him and said, "Guess who!"

He caught his breath, knowing the Indian children would address him in the Shoshonean dialect but this little voice came in clear English. He asked softly, "I don't know, who could it be? Give me a hint?"

The little voice said, "I have red hair!"

Tears came into the eyes of the big Irishman and he lifted

his hands to the little ones at his eyes, slowly turned around and said, "You're my little Sadie!"

The redheaded Irish lass stood smiling, freckles cascading across her nose, and white teeth shining as she said, "Ummmhumm!" and stretched her arms wide to hug her grandpa.

A LOOK AT VENGEANCE VALLEY (ROCKY MOUNTAIN SAINT 8)

Tate Saint, man of the mountains and now a family man, has had more than his share of Indian uprisings and battles, but has always maintained a friendship with many of the native peoples. While in the Sangre de Cristo mountains, he was known and respected by the Comanche and Ute, feared by the Jicarilla Apache, but when the Apache and Ute ally themselves against the white man, Tate becomes concerned for the safety of his family and chooses to move back to the Wind River mountains.

But when he is confronted with the massacre of a wagon train of settlers on the Oregon trail, and is asked by the mountain man scout for General Harney at Fort Laramie, Jim Baker, to scout out the marauding Indians responsible, he accepts the charge, but mainly out of concern for his own family. And that scout brings him up against a blood-thirsty self-appointed war chief of the Crow who is bent on vengeance against any and all whites for what he believes is the attempt to destroy his own people with disease, murder, and by stealing their homelands.

The truth becomes known about this man who has taken the name of a figure from the history of the Crow people and turned it into one of shame, vengeance and blood-letting. It will take an alliance of a group of freighters, a wagon train of settlers, and a party of the traditional enemy of the crow from the Arapaho band of Tate's first wife to bring an end to this vengeance quest by none other than Bad Heart Bear.

AVAILABLE DECEMBER 2018 FROM B.N. RUNDELL AND WOLFPACK PUBLISHING

Born and raised in Colorado into a family of ranchers and cowboys, B.N. Rundell is the youngest of seven sons. Juggling bull riding, skiing, and high school, graduation was a launching pad for a hitch in the Army Paratroopers. After the army, he finished his college education in Springfield, MO, and together with his wife and growing family, entered the ministry as a Baptist preacher.

Together, B.N. and Dawn raised four girls that are now married and have made them proud grandparents. With many years as a successful pastor and educator, he retired from the ministry and followed in the footsteps of his entrepreneurial father and started a successful insurance agency, which is now in the hands of his trusted nephew. He has also been a successful audiobook narrator and has recorded many books for several award-winning authors. Now finally realizing his life-long dream, B.N. has turned his efforts to writing a variety of books, from children's picture books and young adult adventure books, to the historical fiction and western genres.